THE

HIDDEN

CASE

First edition published in 2024
© Copyright 2024
Allison Osborne

The right of Allison Osborne to be identified as the author of this work has been asserted by her in accordance with the Copyright, Designs and Patents Act 1998.

All rights reserved. No reproduction, copy or transmission of this publication may be made without express prior written permission. No paragraph of this publication may be reproduced, copied or transmitted except with express prior written permission or in accordance with the provisions of the Copyright Act 1956 (as amended). Any person who commits any unauthorised act in relation to this publication may be liable to criminal prosecution and civil claims for damage.

All characters appearing in this work are fictitious. Any resemblance to real persons, living or dead, is purely coincidental. The opinions expressed herein are those of the author and not of Orange Pip Books.

Paperback ISBN: 978-1-80424-443-2
ePub ISBN: 978-1-80424-444-9
PDF ISBN: 978-1-80424-445-6

Published by Orange Pip Books
335 Princess Park Manor, Royal Drive,
London, N11 3GX
www.orangepipbooks.com

HOLMES & CO. MYSTERIES

COLLECTION ONE
THE INTRODUCTION OF HOLMES & CO

A STUDY IN VICTORY RED
THE CIRCLE CODE CONUNDRUM
THE IMPOSSIBLE MURDERER
THE HAPPY FAMILY FACADE
THE RED ROVER SOCIETY
THE DETECTIVE'S NEMESIS

COLLECTION TWO
THE ADVENTURES OF HOLMES & CO

THE HIDDEN CASE
THE MISSING TWO
THE AMERICAN VISITORS

It is only goodness which gives extras, and so I say again that we have much to hope from the flowers.

-Sherlock Holmes, *The Adventure of the Naval Treaty*

Chapter I

The Beginnings of a Very Curious Case

Irene Holmes sat on the cushioned chair in her landlady's living room in the bottom flat of 221 Baker Street with a pair of trousers draped over her lap. She scowled at the threaded needle between her forefinger and thumb as she stabbed the fabric. The point poked through and caught her skin, drawing blood. A curse teetered on the tip of her tongue, but she quickly bit it back as that would have her in hot water with Miss Hudson. Instead, she dropped everything on the ground and huffed.

"Pick those up." The older woman chided, white hair bouncing as she nodded to the heap. "And if you throw another fit, you will finish *all* the stitching, not just the one leg."

Arguing with Miss Hudson was futile. All of Irene's trousers needed mending after the rigorous winter that befell London earlier this year. And it wasn't particularly fair to rely on Miss

Hudson to stitch both her *and* Joe's clothing. The winter had also taken its toll on the landlady, and though she remained spry and sharp-witted, she was slowing down as her age – and stress caused by Irene and her antics – caught up to her.

Irene scooped up the trousers again, finding the needle. As much as she wanted to help Miss Hudson, sewing was a most tedious task. Her mind wandered to literally anything and everything else. The needle met skin yet again, causing an involuntary curse under her breath.

Miss Hudson tut-tutted. "You are grand at so many things, Irene Holmes, I know that you can do this."

"Perhaps this is the one task that I lack skill in."

"Nonsense. I know what you're doing. You think that if you do so terribly at this, I will let you off the hook to bury yourself in your chemistry set."

Irene wished that to be true. Of course, she could always try to learn, but she wanted to be good at sewing immediately, and that wasn't happening. Most every other task came easily to her, and those that didn't, she simply didn't pursue.

Sewing, however, was one such activity that would take her more than a day to learn, and therefore was a waste of time.

Miss Hudson nudged her leg. "Carry on."

As Irene started into yet another stitch, the front door to opened and shut. Wellies thumped in the front hall and a sharp bark sounded throughout the halls as Isla, the little West

Highland Terrier, arrived.

Irene instantly perked up, seeing her opportunity to escape the dreadful task.

Miss Hudson was on her immediately though, smacking her leg.

"You stay put."

Irene carefully tied off the needle and thread, folded the pants and placed them gently on the table, all under the stern glare of her landlady.

"Joe is walking with heavy steps," she said, listening as her flatmate thumped up the stairs. "And he is home precisely twenty-seven minutes earlier than usual. Something is wrong, and it's my job to figure out what is troubling my dear friend. I shall finish the trousers, have no fear. But today will not be that day."

Miss Hudson sighed and gave a flick of her wrist. "I'll be up in ten with the tea. If Joe truly had a lousy day, then perhaps meat and potatoes are in order for supper."

"Real potatoes? Not the dreadful ones from the box?"

"Those dreadful ones are the food that's keeping you from fainting in a hungry spell, missy."

Irene grinned at the woman before spinning and heading out of the flat. She paused for a fraction of a second to glance at the wall along the stairs.

The flooding from the melt in the spring had seeped right into the building and left horrid stains. They had pooled their money for replacement rugs and carpeting for the front hall. And while the new carpet looked grand, the inch-high stains remained on the wall.

Irene hurried up the stairs, skipping the squeaky fifth out of habit. Despite her wraith-like ascent, Isla heard her and gave a few excited yips. She crouched to the ground immediately, meeting the little white dog at the top of the stairs.

Isla was full grown now, weighing close to two stone, and – despite Joe bathing her often – her paws and skirt were always singed with London dirt. Much like the hem of Irene's trousers.

She scratched behind the pup's ears, fluffing her face and nose.

"Go find Joe."

The door to the flat lay wide open giving a clear view to half of the sitting room, including Doctor Joe Watson. He sat in his armchair, tall frame splayed out on the cushions, head back and eyes closed. His dark auburn hair stuck out at every strand as if he'd run his hands through it too often.

Isla bounded into the room, leaping onto his lap. He grunted. Just as quickly as she'd pounced, the little white terrier jumped off to run back to Irene.

Joe straightened and gave a disheartened smile when he saw Irene, trying to give the appearance that he was in a better mood.

"How are the trousers coming along?"

She held up her bandaged finger.

"Well, at least you're finished them."

"I am not."

"Then why are you here? I thought you were determined to finish them today."

Irene flopped on the couch. "You are home. How can I concentrate on another task when you are up here all by–"

"Oh no." Joe leaned forward and shook his head. "You are not using me as an excuse to skip out on a lesson with Miss Hudson."

Irene crossed her legs, looking at him in the most attentive manner. "Well, you've had a hard day at work and I simply cannot leave you alone."

"You leave me alone all the time. Besides, you have no obligation to dote on me like that. You're not my wife."

Irene straightened, raising an eyebrow. "You expect your wife to dote on you?"

"What?" He sighed, clearly distracted at whatever thoughts raced through his mind. "No, I don't. I just..."

She frowned at her friend. Joe always seemed to have a million thoughts rushing about in his mind. He was hyper-aware of everyone's feelings and did his best to not tread on anyone. But this all weighed heavily, it was clear. 221B was where he was most relaxed. Yet this evening, something had followed him to his sanctuary.

"Tell me what ails you and I shall do my best to help."

"I am fine."

"Joe," Irene sighed. "Must we go through this back and forth? You are rumpled and ragged. Your right cuff is torn and there is a large splatter of dried blood on your pant leg. Your hair is wilder than the Moors, meaning you've messed it with stress probably every half-hour on the dot."

He stared at her, as he often did, trying to counter the deductions. In the end, though, he let out a great sigh and reached down to pet Isla.

"I lost a patient today. A Great Dane with a bloated belly. And earlier in the morning, a lady could not afford the services needed to fix her dog's leg. I ended up doing the procedure at half cost and told Michael to take the rest out of my payment. He refused, of course, which was kind of him."

"If all of this is about money then–"

"It isn't. I am forever thankful that the rent here is just the cost of upkeep, and I will be eternally grateful to Miss Hudson for being so kind to me. It's..."

He trailed off again and shrugged.

"You wish to eat better food?"

His eyes widened and he looked to the door in a panic. "Goodness no! Don't let Miss Hudson hear you say that."

"You wish to live in a bigger house?"

"Of course not. I truly love living here."

"Would you prefer to work at another vet practice?"

He paused at this suggestion. "There is a nice practice up north. It caters to wealthier clients. Or I could get back into large animal practice. But both of those require travel, and I couldn't possibly take up that much use of the car."

Irene furrowed her brow. "If working at another vet practice, or treating cows, would make you happy, then you can have the car as much as you want. Unless we are on a case, of course."

"Of course." He gave her a tired smile, gazing at her with a certain fondness he only saved for her and Isla.

Irene had yet to decipher what that look meant, but it warmed her heart and made her feel like Joe was truly her best friend.

The best friend in question sighed and ruffled the pup's head before standing. Something on Irene's desk caught his eye as he passed by the window.

"Henriette is visiting London next week?" He lifted a letter from a pile of papers. "Oh, lovely. Are you going to ask her to pop by for tea?"

"Almost certainly."

They'd met Henriette Grouper and her husband during their second case together. The woman had worked for Bletchley Park during the war. She had a knack for puzzles and cyphers, and a level of intelligence that Irene respected.

Over the winter, they'd taken up writing to each other a few times a month, chatting about everything from what they'd done during the war, to politics in the news, or everything new and wonderful in the city.

Irene considered Henriette a friend, even though she felt as though she had enough people's lives to keep up with. Still, she was making an effort. Having someone new to correspond with every month, who could keep up with her intelligence, was pleasant.

Suddenly, Isla leapt up and out of the flat.

"Oh heavens," a voice chided from the hallway. "Get out from under me you little wee hairy bampot."

Miss Hudson stomped about, a tray of food in her hands, as she tried to avoid the dog.

Joe rushed over and scooped Isla out of the way.

Irene laughed. "Miss Hudson, she has no idea what you're saying."

Joe mumbled as he passed his partner. "I have no idea what she's saying either."

Irene tried not to burst out laughing again as she took the tray of food and set it on the table.

Miss Hudson scoffed. "Aye, well she will when I step on her feet and fall on her like a sack of potatoes."

The pair settled into their dinner, grinning at each other, as Miss Hudson scolded the dog then proceeded to pat her and make kissy noises.

* * * * *

The next day, Irene stared up at the ceiling, with Isla tucked beside her on the couch. The dog snored lightly, making tiny barking noises as she dreamed. Irene didn't want to wake the small creature, so she'd stayed put. Not that she had much else to do.

She lifted her right arm straight up, waiting for the pins and needles feeling to start.

"I doubt that's good for your appendages," Joe called from the small kitchen. He had the day off and Irene only now just remembered that he was even home.

"Morning, Joe."

"I'm afraid morning's almost over. I'm off to Sarah's shortly."

"Hm."

Sarah James, Joe's girlfriend of about five months now, had moved into a townhouse with three of her friends a few days ago. They'd asked Joe to come and peruse the property, to ensure everything was satisfactory before they hauled their furniture in.

Irene had quipped that they should've done that before they signed any agreement, but Joe had hushed her.

"Do you know much about craftsmanship?" She called to him.

"Not at all. I can get by with basic knowledge, only because I watched my father do odd jobs at the farm. Even then, I was so distracted by the animals that only some of the lessons stuck."

"So, what are you going to today, then?"

"My best."

Even from her place on the couch, Irene could hear him fidgeting.

"What are *you* doing today?" he asked, clearly stalling for time. "Working on those trousers again?"

She sat up quickly, startling the dog. Poor Isla wiggled and flailed, trying to right herself.

"Do not speak so loud," she snapped, "lest Miss Hudson hear you and drag me downstairs by my ear."

An amused smirk crossed Joe's lips. "I shall try to keep that thought to myself as I head out."

He kept the smirk on his face and gave her a wink despite the glare he received. Irene let out a huff and rolled her eyes, then flopped back on the couch.

"Begone." She waved her hand dramatically, then noticed Isla's tousled fur. "Oh goodness."

Joe chuckled, leaving his flatmate to deal with the dog's rumpled face.

* * * * *

Joe hadn't been gone ten minutes before the doorbell went.

Irene had moved to her desk in an attempt to organize the monumental stack of papers. At the sound of the door, the terrier went mad, barking and rushing toward to the hallway.

"Isla!" Irene shouted. "Quiet!"

The dog silenced, but kept a low growl in her throat.

"Good girl." Irene grabbed a treat from one of the many jars they kept around the flat and fed it to the dog. Joe had all these ideas about dog training and so far, they worked. Except for the stubbornness of terriers, of course, but that was their way, according to the professional veterinarian living in the flat.

The front door creaked as Miss Hudson answered the call.

"Irene!" The landlady's shrill voice rang from the stairs. She stomped up, huffing and puffing, as if carrying something large and heavy.

Irene stood lazily and sauntered to the door. She opened it just as Miss Hudson reached the threshold. A large bouquet of flowers obscured her face.

Irene stepped back, letting her into the flat.

"Oh, aren't these just lovely!"

Miss Hudson set the bouquet on the table, next to a pile of organized papers.

"My work!" Irene rushed forward, scooping the papers lest water splashed onto them. She set them on the couch as Miss Hudson beamed at the arrangement.

A few pink roses were dotted in amongst a bouquet of

carnations and baby's breath. The scent quickly spread through the flat.

Irene raised her brow at the whole grand affair, then plucked the card from the centre.

"This is a bit excessive."

The front had her name scrawled beautifully in expensive pen by a left-handed gentleman. She immediately knew who'd sent these. The message at the back read:

Dearest Irene,

I hope this bouquet finds you well. My offer for dinner still stands should you wish to accompany me.

Yours truly,

Basil

She rolled her eyes. "What am I going to do with these?"

"Display them, of course!" Miss Hudson spun around, looking for a more permanent spot for the large vase.

"I already have flowers on display." Irene gestured to the collection of dying plants by the window. Joe had collected them one day on his way home from work, claiming he'd never seen Irene with flowers before, and perhaps these would brighten up her often dreary-looking desk.

The older woman tsk-tsk'd. "Half of those are weeds."

"Well, I like the look of weeds and wildflowers much better. These look like they belong in the palace, not our well-worn flat."

"Oh, come now." Miss Hudson snatched the card from her and tucked it back into the bouquet. "There must be some feminine part of you that thinks this is ever-so-slightly lovely."

Irene gazed at the flowers, the sickly-sweet scent tickling her nose. She and Basil Cullens had gone to lunch twice, but she'd kept everything casual on both occasions. He'd asked her to dinner, but she knew that inched into the dangerous territory of an actual date. The thought made her weary and nervous all at once.

She sighed, despite herself, and plucked a carnation. These flowers must've been hard to come by, even for a government agent such at Mr. Cullens.

"I suppose I shall write him a thank you note."

The landlady nodded in approval. "That's the right thing to do whether you intend to keep them or not. And if you want rid of them, then I shall take them down to my own place."

With that, Miss Hudson left the flat.

Alone again, Irene sat down at her desk. She poked at the drying purple wildflowers that Joe had brought her as she thought of what words to use for her thank-you note.

After five minutes of staring at the blank stationery, she stood, knocking her chair back. She needed to do something else – something that didn't involve the man who'd sent her flowers. Perhaps she'd wander down to Sarah's new house and see how

Joe was doing with his inspection. She'd bet a crisp tenner that she could offer more information than her oblivious partner could.

With the decision made, she popped into her bedroom and applied lipstick, ran a brush through her hair, and clipped up her dark curls to keep them from blowing around. She spent way too long pondering which hat to wear, and in the end left without one.

"Goodbye, Isla." The dog followed her to the basket by the lavatory where they kept her things and Irene pulled out a hearty bone. "Sit."

When Isla obeyed, Irene handed her the bone and the pup scurried under Joe's desk.

As Irene hurried down the steps, she heard Miss Hudson bustling in the lower hallway.

"Off to mail that thank you note, love?" she called.

Irene winced, having completely forgotten about the note, even in this short time.

"Uh, yes, Miss Hudson!"

"Good lass."

Irene hurried out the door before the older woman could ask any more questions.

London was a soggy mess after the intense winter months. Snow unlike Irene had ever seen before had fallen in waves upon the city, stopping traffic. She was grateful it had all melted, but it left the streets, and all the building repairs, in such a state of disarray.

The taxi dropped her off at the top of the Sarah's street as the driver wanted to avoid the large pothole further down.

Irene paid, then started down the pavement.

All the houses sat in long rows, with small empty gardens out front, connecting to the pavement. Some of them bombed out and some of them were simply in need of general repair.

There were a few dotted throughout that were recently refurbished – diamonds in the rough of the somewhat dilapidated street. Once construction was finished on these houses, they would be quite desirable.

Half a dozen people filled the pavement:

An elderly couple strolling at their leisure.

A young businessman arriving home from work.

And a man, alone, walking deliberately slow.

He piqued her curiosity. She paused, stepping behind a small wall to conceal herself as she watched him. He gazed up at the houses, not looking at anyone in particular. He could've been another passer-by, but he was trying too hard at attempting to amble, planting his feet in a very specific, slow way.

He hesitated in front of every front garden, looking downward at something. The first house seemed to pass whatever inspection and so he moved on to the next.

Irene stepped out from her hiding spot and slowly trailed

behind him, observing as much as she could.

This was an older gentleman, walking with a cane to help with a limp on his right leg. His clothing was slightly big, but might have fit him at an earlier point in time. Under his hat, greying hair suggested he must've fought in the war – unless his injury had prevented him.

The pavement gave no indication of shoe print or size. Irene needed to catch a glimpse of his face or move closer to gain more insight.

But the man kept pausing in front of every house along the street. Soon, they approached Sarah's rented property.

There, he slowed, just like the previous houses, but this time, the cane fell. Irene had no idea how; it was as if the man simply let it fall from his fingers. He stooped to pick it up and hesitated for the briefest moment before carrying on.

He continued in this manner, snooping and peering at the different residences.

Irene set her shoulders. This simply would not do. There was a mystery here, and she was determined to figure out who this man was.

He quickened his steps as he approached the end of the row, and she kept pace. As he moved, he used the cane less and less, until the tip barely touched the ground.

There was a small alleyway up ahead. As soon as he got to it, he pivoted. Irene turned the corner moments behind him and came to an empty dead end.

The alley had wooden crates and bricks piled at the chain fence to the next street over. While she could easily climb up and over to the opposite alley, the supposedly crippled man she observed simply could not.

Something was afoot.

Irene stepped out of the alley, carefully observing the street. After a few moments, she headed to Sarah's house with a newfound determination in her step.

Chapter II

In Search of a Mystery

Joe pursed his lips as he studied the beams running along the walls of the upper bedroom. There were no visible flaws in the wood, though his inexperienced eye didn't quite know what to look out for.

Despite taking the day off to help Sarah, he was heavy-hearted with all the cases that turned sour on him.

In general, the current dreary state of the veterinary world was immensely troubling. Medicines were hard to come by for people, let alone animals. The public's funds had dwindled during the war and, except for the few rich folk who could afford the world, individuals simply did not want to spend the money on their animals when their kids had no food to eat.

He turned to the women in the empty room. Sarah had introduced Maria, Jenny and Dottie before and Joe did his best to remember which one was which, as the three of them seemed to all be together whenever he saw them. Maria had the darkest hair and was suspicious of everything, while Jenny kept her hair quite short and seemed to be in a constant state of confusion. Dottie's hair was blonder than Sarah's and she spoke in a quiet voice.

They all looked at him now as if his word were gospel.

"This place looks good. Solidly made."

A collective sigh of relief echoed through the hollow space.

"Thank you," Sarah said, clutching Joe's hand. "We just don't really trust anyone else. And with our furniture coming this afternoon, we wanted someone to look at it."

"Is there much being delivered?"

"Just our beds and dressers, and a few small tables. The rest will arrive tomorrow. We have a lovely sitting room set from Jenny's parents."

Joe squeezed his girlfriend's hand and gave a reassuring smile.

The girls fanned out to look at the rest of the house, but Sarah stayed back.

"I feel like we haven't seen each other much. You've been so busy."

"Just trying to figure out what to do, I suppose."

"I think going back to vet practice was a good idea. A steady, guaranteed income is perfect for our future."

He swallowed a nervous chuckle. "Exactly."

In truth, Joe didn't feel as confident about anything as he did when he was solving mysteries with Irene. Even his vet skills – though still solid after the war – were not as satisfying as they once were.

But he'd been with Sarah long enough that he did have to think of the future, whatever that may be.

"Joe?"

He blinked, pulling himself back into the present. "Sorry."

Sarah giggled, tucking a piece of blonde hair behind her ear. Standing on her tiptoes, she kissed him on the cheek. "Lost you there for a second."

There was no doubt that Sarah was much prettier than she had the right to in being with Joe. The truth was, he didn't consider himself a particularly handsome man, even though she told him so often. Even Irene complimented his looks. But she also thought fungi and corpses were lovely, so he wasn't sure he trusted her opinion on beauty.

The door downstairs opened and slammed shut, halting these thoughts.

The three women on the lower level went into a flurry of surprised gasps.

Joe was instantly on guard.

He gently nudged Sarah into the corner of the bedroom, putting himself between her and the door. A female voice snapped at the trio downstairs. Heavy footsteps started quickly up the stairs and Joe strode out of the room to meet whoever was in such a hurry.

A familiar figure leapt up the top step, causing a collision. Irene muttered a curse as he grabbed her, preventing a tumble.

Maria huffed her larger frame up the stairs, hollering. "Excuse me. We are looking at this house, thank you very much."

Irene whipped around and snapped at the poor woman. "If you mean that you were gossiping about Joe and Sarah, then you most certainly were very interested."

Joe swallowed a frustrated grumble and steered his flatmate into the first bedroom.

Maria stomped up behind them and addressed Sarah.

"You know her?"

Sarah sighed. "This is Irene."

"Oh. Is that so?"

Joe held his breath, hoping his hot-headed friend would keep focus on what she came in here to say with so much haste instead of getting caught up in an argument. Luckily, she simply raised her eyebrow at Maria, and spun back to Joe.

"I've just followed a strange man down the street." She spoke as if there was no one else in the room.

Sarah stepped up. "Strange man? How do you mean?"

Jenny and Dottie made it up the stairs then and joined the group in the small room.

Having an audience, Irene clasped her hands together and addressed the women. "He walked with a limp and a cane, but had neither an injury nor the need for assistance. He stopped at each house to investigate it more thoroughly than any man I've known."

Everyone besides Joe, who gritted his teeth, let out small gasps. The last thing he needed was a group of panicked women.

As he opened his mouth to offer soothing words, Sarah spoke up.

"Are we in danger?"

Joe shook his head. "No, you are not–"

"Quite possibly," Irene spoke over him.

"Everything is fine," he said as he saw the pairs of widening eyes. "I will take a look down the street when we leave."

"We shall report it to Scotland yard," Irene said.

Joe almost clamped a hand over her mouth. He did see an opportunity, though, to end this panicked conversation.

"We do have friends on the police force," he drawled in an attempt to claim back any authority over the situation. "We shall have them send a constable to patrol the street, just to be sure there are no strange folk about."

He gave a pointed look to Irene, who rolled her eyes as a response. This suggestion seemed to calm the women who began to talk amongst themselves.

Sarah linked her arm in him. "That would be good of you. I'll walk you both out if you've finished the inspection." Joe gave a to all be together whenever he saw them. Maria had the darkest hair and was suspicious of everything, while Jenny kept her hair quite short and seemed to be in a constant state of confusion. Dottie's hair was blonder than Sarah's and she spoke in a quiet voice.

They all looked at him now as if his word were gospel.

"This place looks good. Solidly made."

A collective sigh of relief echoed through the hollow space.

"Thank you," Sarah said, clutching Joe's hand. "We just don't really trust anyone else. And with our furniture coming this afternoon, we wanted someone to look at it."

"Is there much being delivered?"

"Just our beds and dressers, and a few small tables. The rest will arrive tomorrow. We have a lovely sitting room set from Jenny's parents."

Joe squeezed his girlfriend's hand and gave a reassuring smile.

The girls fanned out to look at the rest of the house, but Sarah stayed back.

"I feel like we haven't seen each other much. You've been so busy."

"Just trying to figure out what to do, I suppose."

"I think going back to vet practice was a good idea. A steady, guaranteed income is perfect for our future."

He swallowed a nervous chuckle. "Exactly."

In truth, Joe didn't feel as confident about anything as he did when he was solving mysteries with Irene. Even his vet skills – though still solid after the war – were not as satisfying as they once were.

But he'd been with Sarah long enough that he did have to think of the future, whatever that may be.

"Joe?"

He blinked, pulling himself back into the present. "Sorry."

Sarah giggled, tucking a piece of blonde hair behind her ear. Standing on her tiptoes, she kissed him on the cheek. "Lost you there for a second."

There was no doubt that Sarah was much prettier than she had the right to in being with Joe. The truth was, he didn't consider himself a particularly handsome man, even though she told him so often. Even Irene complimented his looks. But she also thought fungi and corpses were lovely, so he wasn't sure he trusted her opinion on beauty.

The door downstairs opened and slammed shut, halting these thoughts.

The three women on the lower level went into a flurry of surprised gasps.

Joe was instantly on guard.

He gently nudged Sarah into the corner of the bedroom, putting himself between her and the door. A female voice snapped at the trio downstairs. Heavy footsteps started quickly up the stairs and Joe strode out of the room to meet whoever was in such a hurry.

A familiar figure leapt up the top step, causing a collision. Irene muttered a curse as he grabbed her, preventing a tumble.

Maria huffed her larger frame up the stairs, hollering. "Excuse me. We are looking at this house, thank you very much."

Irene whipped around and snapped at the poor woman. "If you mean that you were gossiping about Joe and Sarah, then you most certainly were very interested."

Joe swallowed a frustrated grumble and steered his flatmate into the first bedroom.

Maria stomped up behind them and addressed Sarah.

"You know her?"

Sarah sighed. "This is Irene."

"Oh. Is that so?"

Joe held his breath, hoping his hot-headed friend would keep focus on what she came in here to say with so much haste instead of getting caught up in an argument. Luckily, she simply raised her eyebrow at Maria, and spun back to Joe.

"I've just followed a strange man down the street." She spoke as if there was no one else in the room.

Sarah stepped up. "Strange man? How do you mean?"

Jenny and Dottie made it up the stairs then and joined the group in the small room.

Having an audience, Irene clasped her hands together and addressed the women. "He walked with a limp and a cane, but

27

had neither an injury nor the need for assistance. He stopped at each house to investigate it more thoroughly than any man I've known."

Everyone besides Joe, who gritted his teeth, let out small gasps. The last thing he needed was a group of panicked women.

As he opened his mouth to offer soothing words, Sarah spoke up.

"Are we in danger?"

Joe shook his head. "No, you are not–"

"Quite possibly," Irene spoke over him.

"Everything is fine," he said as he saw the pairs of widening eyes. "I will take a look down the street when we leave."

"We shall report it to Scotland yard," Irene said.

Joe almost clamped a hand over her mouth. He did see an opportunity, though, to end this panicked conversation.

"We do have friends on the police force," he drawled in an attempt to claim back any authority over the situation. "We shall have them send a constable to patrol the street, just to be sure there are no strange folk about."

He gave a pointed look to Irene, who rolled her eyes as a response. This suggestion seemed to calm the women who began to talk amongst themselves.

Sarah linked her arm in him. "That would be good of you. I'll walk you both out if you've finished the inspection." Joe gave a quick glance to his friend, knowing that if he continued to look around the house, she'd just follow him and find a thousand insignificant flaws.

"I am, yes."

"I'll be back, ladies." Sarah addressed her friends, leading the pair down the stairs. Irene ambled behind them as they crossed the empty sitting area and Joe prayed nothing distracted her from leaving. There was no need for another scene.

They exited the house, Irene thankfully in tow, and as they reached the front pavement, Sarah addressed them both. "Tell me honestly. Are we in any danger?"

"No," Joe answered, but Sarah didn't want an answer from him.

To her credit, Irene hesitated before answering.

"Not immediate danger. I chased the man off before he could do anything if he was so inclined. He could have been a scoundrel, or he simply could be a man whose mind has not quite healed from war. But, either way, Joe's idea is a good one. We will have a constable check the streets."

Sarah blew out a relieved breath. "Thank you. And, of course, you both are more than welcome here. There's a lot of us, and they don't warm up well to new friends… But they will come to like you, Irene, I'm sure."

"Of course."

Joe could tell his friend had already moved on to other

matters.

Sarah left to rejoin the group inside. As soon as she was gone, Joe turned to Irene, but she held up a hand.

"I know what you're going to say, and you are correct. I am over-cautious and find suspicion in almost every event. But I think it is warranted this time."

He couldn't argue, but still offered his own thoughts. "This man could've just been nosy about four pretty women moving into a house together. Men tend to have a one-thought mind sometimes."

"Almost all the time," Irene quipped. "And I would've thought the same, but he was stopping at every house, Joe. Dropping his cane and stalling to get a better look at each."

She held her hand out. He fished the car keys from his pocket and dropped them in her palm. As soon as the metal jingled in her fingers, she headed to the 37' Vauxhall parked up the street.

Joe followed, resigned to the day's new plan. Not that he was doing much else.

While Irene's claim to this mysterious man could be valid, it was no secret to anyone that she was desperate for a case, no matter how trivial. Especially after the cold winter they spent shut in 221B.

Irene stopped at the car and opened the driver's door. She peered dramatically down the street as if waiting for some scoundrel to pop out.

"Strange things are afoot today, Joe."

The doctor sighed, climbing in the passenger seat. "No, they are not."

Within seconds, the engine rumbled and took them toward Scotland Yard.

* * * * *

Irene parked a little too close to a Wolseley police car, but cut the engine before Joe had time to open his mouth in concern. He jogged to catch her as she hurried up the front steps.

The pair entered the bustling building and only a few faces looked at them in question. By now, Irene and Joe frequented Scotland Yard often enough that only rookies or supervisors who didn't know them well took issue with the visits.

Irene weaved in and out of desks, aiming for one of the back offices. Joe followed, twisting and turning. He mumbled a few apologies at the constables that Irene passed, accidentally knocking their things as she went.

Detective Inspectors Eddy Lestrade and Thom Gregory stood in their shared office, each with a cup of tea. Joe wished he could signal a warning about the force that was Irene Holmes today, but she stormed in ahead.

Lestrade noticed her first, mid-conversation with his partner.

"Oh dear. We are in fine form today."

The detective was almost as tall as Joe, but not as lanky. He had the worn look of a man that had seen plenty in life. Considering he'd been friends with Irene since childhood, the look fit. His long face was usually clean-shaven, but now sported a moustache.

"We may have a mystery on our hands, gentlemen," Irene said, then recoiled at her friend's face. "Oh my. It looks as though a caterpillar has taken up residence."

Gregory slapped his desk. "I told you, Ed. Some of us aren't meant to have facial hair. Personally, it would cover my beautiful skin quite fetchingly, but in your case, it appears as if you are going to rob a bank."

Poor Lestrade only shook his head. "Regardless of your thoughts on my appearance, what are you so fired up about?"

Irene set her shoulders, ready to tell her tale. Behind her, Joe shook his head at the detectives, attempting to tell them that what they were about to hear was dramatized to no end.

His partner must've sensed his movement, because she waved him off.

"Pay no mind to Joe," she said, calling their attention back.

She quickly told them about the man on the street, emphasizing the strangeness of it all.

Joe sighed, listening, but not finding anything truly odd.

When she was finished, Irene waited for both men's reactions.

They simply stared.

"Apologies, Irene," Lestrade started, "but I don't see how that's grounds for opening a case."

"But it is! This man–"

"Was walking down the street," Gregory interrupted. "Many of them have only been back a year after spending the majority of their adult life fighting a war."

"Or he was simply viewing the new construction," Lestrade offered.

Scowling, Irene folded her arms.

Gregory mirrored her expression and turned to his desk, poking at some papers.

Meanwhile, Lestrade looked exasperated, but tried his best to soothe his long-time friend.

"Are you trying to find a case where there isn't one?"

"Yes," Joe said.

"No," Irene shot back.

The DI and sleuth were now caught in a staring match. Irene was determined to solve a case, even if it were a figment of her imagination.

Gregory turned back to them, a report in his hand.

"There was one break-in last week. Right down the street from where you saw that man. But that's not out of the ordinary. Times are tough and people are desperate to gather anything they can by any means necessary. Now, we have actual police work to do, so take this to satisfy your cravings for crime-solving and return it tomorrow when you determine that there is nothing strange going on."

Irene looked like she wanted to argue, but plucked the paper from the Inspector's hand before striding out of the office.

"Thank you," Joe said to them. "She's been itching to do something since the weather has turned for the better."

Gregory laughed and stuck a cigarette in his mouth. "We have plenty of cases of our own for her to look through if she wants."

Lestrade scoffed. "You think regular police work would satisfy Irene Holmes?"

"Of course not. But I'd love to get some of these off my desk."

All three of the men laughed.

"Thank you for trying, either way," Joe said. "Cheers."

He hurried out of the precinct in case Irene drove away without him. It hadn't happened yet, but he wouldn't put it past his partner to simply be so involved with her own thoughts that she'd forget him.

Irene was already in the car when he approached, but luckily hadn't started the engine. As soon as Joe climbed in the passenger side, the report smacked him in the face.

"This is useless. A break-in at an empty house with no clues! I should just throw it out the window."

Joe took the paper before it could crinkle any more in her palm. "That is an official police document. It needs to stay *inside* the car."

"I need something sweet. Let's either stop at the bakery on the way home or you ask Miss Hudson to bake us something."

"Why do *I* need to ask?"

Irene stuck the keys in the ignition. "Because if I go near her, she will catch me and make me mend some trousers. And this is no time for sewing."

"What is it time for?"

"Eating sweets and pondering."

With that, they headed toward Baker Street.

Chapter III

A Break-in at the Townhouse

Irene shoved another Turkish Delight into her mouth and sighed, spraying the fine white powder all over the table in their kitchenette. The mess gave pause to Joe's strides.

"Chin up, Irene." He wiped the powder with his hand. "Something will come along. I know the inspectors have a tall pile of cases that they–"

"Mediocre at best, Joe. Dreadfully boring at worst."

"What about that Mr. Cullens fellow? Surely he has something you can assist with."

"That would require Irene to actually speak with the man." Miss Hudson came through the door with a tray of tea.

"Oh?" Joe took the tray and made up the cups. "I thought you were getting quite friendly with him."

"She can barely write him a thank-you note for flowers."

"Perhaps my personal life should stay as such," Irene snapped, then sipped loudly at her tea.

Miss Hudson raised her hands in surrender and turned to leave. "And don't think I've forgotten about those trousers, Miss Holmes."

Irene slurped in answer.

Joe shut the door gently after the landlady. "There is still the possibility of a murder."

Irene perked up. "There is? Of whom?"

"Of us if Miss Hudson finds out how much we spent on these sweets."

Irene scowled, snatching another Turkish Delight. But she couldn't help the smile that tugged her lips.

* * * * *

After tea, Irene resigned to her room. Heaps of books were strewn across the floor. She plopped down to organize the chaos, only pausing for dinner, then went right back to her task as darkness fell upon London.

Finally, when there were half a dozen neat and sorted piles, she stood, unable to take the menial task any longer. There had to be something else to do. She secured her hair back and pulled on a snood and a hat, ensuring not one curl fell. She changed her outfit for the evening, opting for a tighter sweater and snug trousers.

Once satisfied with her clothing choice, she grabbed her favourite sleuthing bag – an old leather-strapped, canvas pack from the first war. The worn bag that once belonged to Eddy's father when he served always housed the essentials: a small knife, a torch, one of the half dozen pairs of handcuffs she'd nicked from Scotland Yard, some fingerprint powder, and a small notebook. She kept the pack stocked so she could grab it and go quickly.

As she slung the strap over her shoulder, she paused. Perhaps it was a wise idea to ask Joe to join. She peeked out and noticed him half asleep, digesting a novel in his chair.

She decided against it. He'd simply roll his eyes and try to convince her not to go. Irene opened the door and hurried across the room.

"I shall be back," she said, quickly tugging on her boots with the softer heel.

"Where are you going?"

"Just for a walk. To think."

Joe finally looked up from his novel. "Alone at night? Do you want company?"

"It is hardly night. And no need. I am content on my own."

If Joe responded, she didn't hear as she hurried down the stairs. That was certainly not the smoothest exit she'd ever made, but hopefully he just went back to his book.

Irene opted to take a taxi, telling the driver to park a block away. The Vauxhall could be a liability as someone might recognize it or even steal it.

There was, however, the possibility of Joe following her. She'd almost swiped the car keys, but that seemed cruel. Joe would need the car to take Miss Hudson to get proper care if she were to get injured, or if there was some other emergency.

Irene paid the driver and headed down the pavement, determined to find a case in this snooping man and the break-in at the empty townhouse a few doors down from Sarah's place. Of course, her friends could be correct and there may not be one at all, but if there was one thing her father taught her, it was to see things through. Sherlock was never one for gut instinct and thought everything needed a reason, but Irene had come to learn that her gut would often lead her to those reasons.

Miss Hudson called it woman's intuition because 'women always know the goings on'. Irene didn't completely disagree, as women often knew more than they thought they did. However, they were the first ones to keep things quiet, lest they get themselves or others they care about in trouble.

She strolled down the street, eyes moving from one house to another. The empty buildings were filling up quickly with patrons looking for housing as London expanded.

After a few minutes, Sarah's house came into view.

Irene cast a curious glance. Almost all the lights were on with female silhouettes breaking up the glow. That was unwise. She'd have to tell Joe to inform them to get proper curtains to keep any Nosey Nellies or Peeping Toms from getting a free show.

When she'd lived with Eddy's sister, Marla, before the war, she'd caught someone outside their house, with a pair of binoculars no less. Grabbing a brolly, Irene had run outside, swinging it around, striking the culprit more than a few times. She still wasn't sure whether it was the hits or the vicious flurry of curse words freely flowing from a woman's delicate mouth that had scared him off more. They'd called Eddy anyway, even after Irene insisted that the man wouldn't come back.

As capable as Sarah and her friends seemed – they had made it through the war, after all – Irene doubted they'd hold their own against a vagrant.

She carried on to her target a few doors down, keeping a close watch on anyone passing by to avoid any unnecessary attention.

Not that it would stop her anyway.

She'd tucked the police report in her pocket. Should any constable question her, Irene could confidently make an argument as to why she was sneaking around a house that was part of an investigation.

As she approached the empty building that had been broken into, she hoped that the front door would be unlocked.

Luckily for her, it opened with ease. Entering the property, Irene checked the hinges and clasp. No sign of forced entry, which meant that either the lock was picked or the door was left open. No damages were stated in the police report; the culprit was probably a homeless man looking for a place to rest for the night and scoop up anything left lying around.

Focusing on the first floor, she looked in the empty kitchen and living area, which showed no signs of disturbance. Just cobwebs and footprints from heavy police boots.

What was even more curious was that nothing was touched. No cupboards opened. No closets left ajar from prying eyes.

Perhaps the upstairs would be more fruitful.

Irene tested each stair before putting any weight on. First step was clear, no creaks. The second step made the slightest noise, but it took her whole weight. The third step, however, groaned as soon as her toe touched it. Skipping this one, she proceeded up the rest.

The upper level had seen more foot traffic than downstairs, which was also curious. No constable footprints, just the same long boots, back and forth between the three bedrooms.

Irene decided to start with the smaller bedroom at the front of the house. As she stepped in, a creak and a faint rush of wind came from down the stairs. Someone else had entered the house and shut the door behind them as silently as possible.

Her entire body froze in an instant and her hearing fine-tuned itself to every move downstairs. Whomever this newcomer was, their attempt to be as silent as possible worked. They moved around the lower level before starting up the stairs, causing the third stair to squeak.

Irene pressed herself against the wall just inside the bedroom door. The man – judging by the heavier footsteps – stopped in the first bedroom, then came toward the front room.

She let out a slow, calming breath as the intruder came around the corner. She went right for his arm and twisted it behind his back. He let out a cry and wiggled, but to no avail. With her free forearm, against the back of his neck, Irene pressed him into the dark wood with all her weight.

As she was about to demand a name from this man, she caught a whiff of cologne that had lingered from a few nights ago.

"Joe! What on earth are you doing here?"

She released him and stepped back, giving him space to turn around. Her friend rotated his shoulder as best as he could and she could just make out the wincing expression.

"I could ask you the same question."

"I am investigating."

"So am I. More specifically, I'm following you. Why did you come here by yourself?"

"To see why the man broke into this house."

"Without me?"

"Evidently not."

Joe pinched the bridge of his nose. Even in the shadows, Irene could see his slumped posture and hear the irritation in his voice.

"You came to an empty house, where a madman had previously broken into, by yourself."

Irene knew what point he was trying to make. Truthfully, it wasn't one of her wisest moves. But instead of admitting her mistake, she grew defensive.

"It was late and I doubt you would've wanted to come with me." She turned away, hoping to have the last word and continue her investigation, but with no such luck.

"I would've come with you had you asked." Joe's words were quiet but poignant.

Irene faltered. He was correct, of course. He would jump off a bridge with her if she asked. That kind of loyalty made her squirm so she pushed the thought aside.

"Regardless. Did you find anything in your investigation?"

He shrugged, regaining his typical demeanour. "Nothing of note. A few broken items, but no carpet pulled up and nothing seemingly stolen. But I suppose I've missed everything?"

She laughed. "Not at all, Joe. There was nothing to see downstairs, which is curious in of itself."

"How do you mean?"

She began to pace, footsteps creaking. "If I were a simple burglar, I would've grabbed something or looked in places conducive to a robbery. The cupboard beneath the stairs was untouched as were the ones in the kitchen. Whoever it was came right upstairs."

"That must mean they were looking for something specific. Or knew where valuables were."

"I'm willing to bet on the first option, my dear Joe." Irene fished the torch from her bag and flicked the light on, shining it around the room. There was nothing but cobwebs.

Joe followed her into the small closet but again, nothing disturbed. They found more of the same in the other bedrooms: evidence of someone walking around, but no secret doors or hidden crevices. He even pushed on the back of each closet, giving the wood a good shove.

After testing the final one, he sighed. "I see nothing."

"There *is* nothing. The man looked around and left. Exactly like the police report states."

Joe gently squeezed his friend's shoulder. "I'm sorry, Irene. Perhaps this is just one to give up on."

Her shoulders slumped and Joe gave another comforting squeeze.

"I just thought there was something here."

"I know. Let's go home. I'll put on a fire and start on a new book. Perhaps Lassie? Or the one I was telling you about the farm animals turning against their farmer. That might be a fun read."

She nodded again and started out of the room and down the stairs. A night in might be just the thing.

She and Joe spent many cold nights over the winter in their

chairs, wrapped up in blankets. He would choose a book to read aloud. Irene found his voice surprisingly soothing and was fond of the inflections he would put on for each character. It was also the only way she consumed fiction stories any more, and was glad Joe had no qualms about sharing his voice.

Once out of the property, Irene spotted the Vauxhall resting against the kerb a few houses up. A small smile passed over her lips. She was grateful that her friend seemed to know her that well.

A gaggle of giggles caught Irene's attention. There was Sarah and her three friends, all dressed for the evening, stepping onto the pavement. Their long coats were pristine and almost identical. Irene couldn't help but think of her own, the hem brushed with dirt, and a small tear in the sleeve.

Sarah noticed them and called their names. Joe stiffened next to Irene.

"What are you two doing here?"

"Investigating," Irene said. "And coming up empty-handed I'm afraid."

One of the women stuck her hip out and folded her arms across her chest. "Investigating late at night together?"

Another elbowed her. "Maria, c'mon."

"It's our job," Irene stated matter-of-factly.

She knew exactly what Maria implied but had no time for such trivial rumours.

Sarah stepped forward, realizing the implication as well. "That's unfortunate that you didn't find any clues. We were just going out dancing...if you'd like to join?"

For a very brief moment, Irene was too surprised to speak. This was the last thing she expected. Well, perhaps she shouldn't have as the woman made many efforts to kindle a friendship with her boyfriend's flatmate. Irene thought of that green dress Joe had given her for Christmas hanging in her closet, and how she hadn't worn it since New Year's.

Then, she caught sight of Maria rolling her eyes, clearly displeased with Sarah's choice, which solidified her decision.

"I do not. But I'm sure I would've had a lovely time. If you are so inclined, go to *Marcel's*. Tell the doorman that Louise Leckie sent you and that you must be treated as a special guest."

"Who is Louise Leckie?" The same woman who chided Maria asked.

"Me, of course. Or who he thinks I am, at least. Do not give him my real name as I would like to keep that cover."

All the women were silent for a brief moment. Sarah was the first to find her words.

"Oh wow. Thank you, Irene. You sure you won't come?"

"Indeed. I have a lot to ponder about this case. Plus, I am hungry and will not dance on an empty stomach."

"Okay. Thank you. Have a lovely night."

Irene nodded her goodbye and continued past them. The rest

also mumbled their thanks.

As Joe passed Sarah, he gave her a peck on the cheek. Irene heard the small gasps of excitement from the girls and moved quicker.

Joe caught up to her. "I'm proud of you."

"Oh?"

"You declined that offer to dance in a very nice manner and you even let them use your name."

"Fake name."

"Either way, well done. You are learning how to interact with society properly."

"Ha," she said. "It is only a means to an end. Could you imagine if I had gone dancing?"

"Do you dance?"

A brief flash of a memory scurried through her mind: Uncle John attempting to teach her the most basic steps and giving up. Her father had eventually explained the techniques in a scientific way. This helped her teach Eddy how to dance before his first date as teenagers.

"I do. And if I recall, you've said you are a dancer too."

In the moonlight, she saw his face flush. "I can... Well... Okay, yes I am a good dancer, if I may boast."

She linked their arms. "You may always boast to me, Joe."

* * * * *

The loud sharp ring of the telephone jolted Irene awake. Above her, Joe thumped out of bed and she calculated if he would make it down the stairs before she could make it out of the covers. The bed sheets were tangled around her legs as a result of a rough night's sleep. She kicked them around as Joe clambered down the stairs, the phone still shrieking.

Finally freed from the malicious sheets, Irene fell out of bed with a loud thud. She grabbed her robe and tugged it on as she stepped out into the sitting area.

"Sarah," Joe said in a soothing tone. "It's alright. Is anyone hurt?"

Irene was instantly on guard and rushed forward, softly colliding with her friend. He bent a little, allowing her to listen in.

"We're fine." The woman's frightened voice came through. "Everyone is fine."

"We'll be over as soon as we can. Turn on the lights and stay together in one room. And do not touch anything."

Joe set the receiver down. "Someone broke into their flat. He's gone now, but they are all very shaken."

Irene did her best to hide the smile peeking through but failed.

"I'll put on some trousers, then."

Chapter IV

A Mystery Presents Itself

As soon as Irene parked the car at the kerb, Joe flung his door open. He bounded across the small front garden to Sarah's house when he noticed Irene was no longer behind him. Instead, she was crouched in the garden, studying the ground.

"Go. I have things to observe out here first."

Joe nodded a response, then entered the house. "Sarah?"

"Up here!" Her shaky voice came from one of the second-level bedrooms.

Joe took the stairs two at a time. He found the four women huddled together. Maria and Jenny had tear stains on their cheeks, but Dottie and Sarah had put on brave faces.

As soon as she saw Joe, however, Sarah flung herself into his arms, burying her face in his shoulder.

"You are safe now." He looked around the now furnished room.

Sarah's small bed stuck out from the wall, while her dresser sat across, next to the closet.

As Sarah clung to Joe, with his arms around her waist holding her close, the whole scene felt a bit intimate to have an audience. The three other women looked on as if in need of an embrace as well and it made his cheeks warm.

"Joe?" Irene thankfully called from the first floor.

"We're all up here."

"You may come down now. I have finished my investigation." Joe ushered the women downstairs. Within a few minutes, everyone was sitting in the living room and Sarah had put the kettle on.

A couch sat against the window, with two mismatched armchairs on either side of the fireplace. Irene paced the room, but as soon as Joe took up a spot in the small armchair, she perched on the armrest, ready to listen.

A few of the women gave her an odd look, but they didn't get a chance to comment.

"I can tell you one thing," Irene started. "Actually, I can tell you several things, but the most important is that the intruder is the same man I followed down the street a few nights ago *and* who broke into the house a few doors down."

Dottie gasped. "Are we in danger?"

Joe leaned forward to address everyone. "No–"

"Possibly," Irene interjected.

He gently nudged his partner. She shifted slightly at his touch, but seemed not otherwise affected by his silent chastising.

She did start pacing again, though. "We will not flatter you with the idea that he is targeting solely you. In fact, I don't think he means harm, simply fear-mongering. But for what purpose? There seems to be a pattern formulating. This man is clearly looking for something. The question is what."

Joe knew that Irene was simply asking questions out loud to appease her own thoughts, but that's only because he knew her well. The worried women sitting in front of them, however, had their eyebrows pinched in search for possible answers. In her element, Irene didn't notice. She settled on the armrest again.

"Tell me exactly what happened; leave nothing out."

Everyone looked at Sarah, who seemed to be holding together the best.

"We were all in bed," she began, sipping at her tea. "And as per Joe's suggestion, we double-bolted the door. When Jenny heard the first bolt open, she woke Dottie. The second bolt was forced, then we heard the door creak. Everyone came to my room as soon as we heard the footsteps downstairs. I yelled at whomever it was to go away. At first, he didn't. He stomped around in confusion a bit and even came to the bottom of the stairs. I yelled that was ringing Scotland Yard. That seemed to do the trick. He cursed and–"

"You heard him speak?" Irene slid off the armrest and stood at full attention.

"Yes. Only a few extremely foul words, though."

"What was his voice like? Be precise."

Sarah looked at the other women but they all shrugged.

"Angry," she said finally. "London accent, possibly south? It was rough, like he needed a lozenge."

Irene clasped her hands together. "Brilliant, Sarah. Excellent observation."

"Oh, thank you." She seemed genuinely flattered at the compliment and Joe couldn't help but smile. Irene didn't hand out compliments easily.

"What happens now?" Dottie asked.

"We make sure a constable is on this street at all hours. And we have some research to do," Irene looked at Joe. "I am very curious as to who used to live in these houses. Perhaps that will give us a clue as to why they are of such interest to this man. Now, we shall bid you good night."

She turned in a flurry, coat flapping out behind her.

Joe stood and nodded to the women. "Lock the door and don't fret. We will solve this case."

Outside, he heard the Vauxhall engine roar to life.

Sarah stood to walk him to the door. "You sure we'll be okay?"

He planted a soft kiss on her lips. "Yes. You know Irene. We'll probably have this solved by tomorrow evening."

The young lady nodded but he knew she wasn't quite

convinced.

Behind him, the engine shifted into gear as Irene, energized with the case, put the car in drive.

Joe waited until Sarah stepped inside and locked the door before heading over.

* * * * *

The library was buzzing that afternoon. While it still was quiet, and empty tables and aisles were still very prominent, people flocked due to the nicer weather.

Joe was grateful for the steady hum and whispered conversations; the noise kept him awake.

He pulled yet another record from the large bin of folders that they'd retrieved from the public archives. In fact, the table's entire surface was covered in boxes and stacks of papers. While Joe tried to keep his work area tidy, Irene's was as messy as ever and completely unorganized. He was certain, though, she knew where each askew paper was, and its place in her research.

His partner's head was drooping. Propping herself up on one hand, she squeezed her eyes shut for a moment, then popped them open, blinking rapidly.

Joe frowned as he headed toward her.

He'd taken a lovely nap when they'd returned home from Sarah's place in the morning, and he'd highly suggested that

Irene do the same. When he'd come downstairs a few hours later, though, she was perched in front of their board, staring at all the written clues.

Now she was no doubt fighting a headache. The bags under her eyes were noticeable from afar.

As if on cue, Irene stood to stretch. A low groaning noise, similar to Isla the dog, escaped her lips as she threw her hands in the air.

Joe sighed and handed her a file. "I wish you would go home and rest."

She set it down on the table, leaning on her knuckles to read it.

"I am fine. I will sleep tonight."

Joe leaned forward too, covering the contents of the folder with his hand.

"You promise? Or do I have to tuck you in myself?"

Irene looked up at him with a familiar scowl, their noses almost touching.

But instead of snapping or rolling her eyes, her expression softened. Her gaze ran across his face and back to his eyes. As if struck with electricity, she straightened and folded her hands across her chest in a defiant stance.

"You should save that kind of talk for your girlfriend."

Joe's cheeks instantly warmed, but he raised a brow. "I didn't think I said anything offensive."

"Oh, you did not. But others might think differently."

"Since when did you care about others' opinions?"

Irene shrugged and leaned back on the table. "Since I started paying more attention to the minute and subtle ways women communicate with each other. It is fascinating."

"Don't you communicate the same way?"

"Perhaps. But I mostly converse with men. And when I do converse with women, I have no one watching me as intently as I watch others."

Joe shrugged, unsure where this was headed. "I could watch you."

Irene huffed at the file. "Would you even know what to observe?"

"I suppose not."

"Exactly," she said, eyes skimming the pages. "It is fine. I will be acutely aware of myself. Now, we must finish our work."

Had he offended her? She'd never reacted that way about his teasing before. Perhaps his friend was genuinely concerned with how others saw her...or rather, their relationship.

Suddenly, Irene gasped and grasped his arm. "Joe, you've done it!"

"What have I done?"

"You found our mystery woman! Well, the one who used to occupy Sarah's house."

The document she held out was a rental agreement between the landlord and three women named Olivia Bennett, June

Harriott, and Carrie Harrison.

"We must find these women and see if they know who might have reason to break into the house."

"And how do we do that?"

"We assume their husbands went into the war. And if the ladies lived in those houses, their men must have made good money – so, officers and above. We pull the awards and medals lists and start with last names. Then, we try the killed-in-action lists. We can also call the landlord and see if he remembers these tenants."

"That's going to take a while. You sure you'll make it?"

She nodded, yet her right eyelid twitched.

"Irene..."

She rubbed her forehead, irritating the skin. "Alright, I'll admit it. I am tired. Are you happy?"

"Yes. We have the name, so let's go home and rest–"

"Oh, no." Irene shook her head. "We are not giving up now that we're so close."

"Close to what? We have a massive list of names to go through."

"Yes, but once we find the women, with or without their husbands, then we can discover why they left the house and why someone might want to break in. Perhaps it's even one of their husbands or kin causing such a ruckus."

"Lower your voice. We are still in the library. I understand your…"

He trailed off because Irene was no longer listening to him. She was looking around fervently, the way she did when she suspected they were being watched.

Joe instantly went on alert. Was there someone to be aware of? He glanced around but could only see other library patrons engrossed in their activities.

"Straighten up that pile," Irene hissed. "And when I come back to you, we are leaving, briskly."

"Are we in danger? What is going on?"

"No danger. Just mind the piles, Joe." She whirled away and headed toward the shelves of boxes.

As she rifled through them, the doctor tidied up their mess. He had no idea what the plan was, but hoped that his partner had come to her senses. As he finished up tucking the last pile in the box, Irene reappeared beside him.

"I've got what we need," she whispered. "Let's go."

Joe stared at her for a moment before realizing what she meant.

"Oh, Irene. You can't take documents from the library. Sarah works here, remember?"

"Don't worry, we'll return them as soon as we are done." She turned to hurry away but Joe caught her arm.

"And should someone else come looking for them?"

Irene raised a dark brow. "You saw the thick layer of dust on them. Those files hadn't been touched since they entered the library. Oh! Grab those newspapers too. We shall walk out casually and no one will question us."

Joe made a point of looking at the large table, then back at his unreasonable companion. "And how is taking these back to Baker Street going to help us?"

"Because I will sleep as you sort them and attempt to match names."

That was sound logic. If Joe insisted they stay here, she would eventually fall asleep on the desk. However, if they took the documents home, they'd be risking trouble, but Irene would sleep.

He shoved the papers under his arm and gestured to the exit.

* * * * *

Almost two hours later, Irene slept soundly on the couch with Isla tucked up beside her. Meanwhile, Joe sat at the dining table, attempting to use the small space to his advantage and wished he had room to spread the papers like at the library. But his friend needed to rest more than he needed the space.

He had made tremendous progress. He scribbled some more notes down in his book and flipped a newspaper article to the *Keep* pile, deeming it important enough to show Irene when she woke.

As if on cue, the slumbering sleuth groaned and shifted on the couch. Isla jumped down and stretched her little legs, tail wagging. Irene's eyes were still half closed, and her hair was flat against her head on the right side. She slid off the couch, scratched Isla's ears, and shuffled over to Joe.

Whatever Irene was worried about regarding their relationship must've vanished when they walked into the flat as now she was tucked up close to him as she always was when working a case.

"Tell me what you've found, my dear Joe."

He reached for the keep pile. "This particular row of houses was occupied by government officials and wealthy wives of officers, which is what we suspected."

He fanned out the rental agreements and lists.

"I also found a Hubert Harriott on the list of medal recipients, the same spelling as the June Harriott on the original rental agreement."

Irene straightened, eyes wide open as she poked through the papers. "I am impressed. This is all fantastic work. So, we have a soldier to speak to."

"Precisely. And thank you. But, there is something more. The officer, Hubert, ended up in a POW camp and was rescued, however, the details are blurry at best. There's no one credited for it; just an article saying they were brought home safe. Usually, when there is a rescue, especially of an officer, it's made a big deal. So, why the secrecy?"

"Why indeed…"

Joe watched Irene for a moment as she scoured the pile of papers. He'd had a thought as soon as she'd fallen asleep that almost deterred him from all his research, and he'd contemplated waking her, but decided against it. Even now, he hesitated, knowing it would cause either an argument or a dismissal.

He said her name cautiously.

She caught his tone and looked sideways. "Yes?"

"Are we sure this is even a case? Obviously, there is something odd going on, but during the war there were many unconventional happenings. Perhaps we are simply intruding into people's personal lives. There could be a thousand reasons for this situation to come to fruition, and I fear that we may reach a dead end should we keep pursuing it."

To his surprise, Irene sighed and nodded. "That thought had crossed my mind as well. But the least we can do is talk to the officer. I promise, if there is no case, I will pack up and return all the papers. Then, maybe we will see if Eddy or Thom have anything for us."

Joe gave her shoulders a quick squeeze. "Jolly good. That was a very mature answer."

"That is both a compliment and an insult."

He released her, giving her a small, playful shove. "What should we tackle now?"

"The couch. For the other half of my nap and to ponder on the information you have given me. We shall visit the soldier tomorrow as it is Saturday and he's most likely to be at home."

* * * * *

The next day, Joe left mid-morning to have lunch with Sarah before he embarked on his afternoon journey with Irene.

He and his girlfriend sat across from one another, enjoying a lovely fish-and-chip lunch. Sarah talked about her friends and dancing and the new store being built just down the street. Joe nodded at the appropriate spots, but his mind was elsewhere.

It had been a long winter, he realized, and he surprisingly missed solving mysteries with Irene.

"What do you think?"

Sarah's question snapped his mind back to the present. He stammered over his words as he attempted to recall the topic at hand.

"I think…"

Sarah sighed but the smile remained. "Sometimes I do wonder where your mind goes, but then I remember that when you are on a case, you are fully consumed by it."

"I am sorry," Joe said softly. "This wasn't supposed to even be one, but it is turning out to be more complicated than simply a strange man wandering about. Now there is your safety to be concerned about and–"

"There are constables patrolling our street. Plus, it's the four of us in the house. We can all take care of each other. Though, I do wish sometimes that I had Irene's boldness."

Joe chuckled. "Sometimes it is not a positive trait. That boldness lands her in trouble often."

Sarah smiled at her plate. "The house we are in right now is suitable for us, but I would love to eventually get out of the city. A small farmhouse would be quite fetching, I think."

Joe nodded. "There are some lovely little houses just outside of London. Irene and I saw a few on a case before Christmas. None of them were for sale, mind you. But that doesn't mean there wouldn't be some in the future."

Sarah perked up at his words. "So, you would be open to living somewhere other than London?"

His chest tightened. Clearing his throat, he sipped at his water.

"Eventually, I suppose," he said, hoping his voice stayed steady. "But there are many more things I want to accomplish before I leave the city."

His mind started to spiral. He'd never given much thought to anything other than life at Baker Street, and he certainly didn't want to think about it right now. He cleared his throat again.

Sarah hadn't said anything more and he felt a wee bit guilty. He decided to change the subject.

"How are your friends fairing in the new home? Not counting the recent events, of course."

Sarah seemed slightly dejected but answered nonetheless. "It is nice for us to be out of our parents' homes. Jenny's fiancé was killed in action, so she sometimes still weeps for him. Maria had a man that she met just last year, but he wasn't quite right in the head. They didn't work out, but he kept pursuing her until it got dangerous. I'm not sure when she saw him last…"

If Sarah said anything more, Joe didn't hear her.

Since he began solving cases with Irene, he'd been getting better at putting his brain in crime-solving mode. As soon as a disgruntled former boyfriend came up, he felt like a hound finally picking up a scent.

"Sarah." He leaned forward a little. "Do you remember the fellow's name? Maria's boyfriend?"

The space between her eyebrows pinched but she nodded her head. "Matthew Stroll. I only met him twice. He adored Maria a bit too much."

"Do you know his occupation? Or if he had been arrested before? Or even where he may be currently? Did he lay hands on her?"

Sarah blinked like a startled animal.

Joe suddenly felt like Irene, hauling inquiries at people regardless of how it would make them feel.

She finally regained her composure and smiled. "I'm not sure where he works. I believe he's been arrested before. You don't think this could all be him, do you? Surely he wouldn't be so elusive if he was trying to reconnect with her?"

"I am not sure. Troubled and rejected minds work in odd ways."

This may have solved the entire case. Perhaps there was no scandalous spy story – just a man who didn't know when to stop.

If this Stroll fellow had been arrested before, then Scotland Yard would have a record of him. Joe would have to pick up Irene first before he went down there–

"You want to leave, don't you?" Sarah's voice broke his thought spiral. There was a bitter tinge to her tone, but well disguised.

"No, no. Of course not."

The woman looked like she wanted to say more, but dabbed her mouth with her napkin. "I'm all finished and must get home to mend some curtains. You may go off."

Both of them stood.

"Sarah..."

She gave him a gracious smile. "This is important to you. And I want this matter to end so I can live peacefully in my new house with my friends. So, go on to Irene and solve this mystery."

She stepped around the table and gave him a kiss on the cheek before tugging her gloves. Joe stared after his girlfriend for a moment as she walked away, frustrated that he'd made such a blunder. As he dug some money from his pocket, he tried to flip his brain like a light switch.

He would purchase some flowers and apologize later, but right now he needed to get back to 221B and relay the new information to his partner.

He couldn't help the grin spreading across his face as he headed home. Leave it to Irene to make a case out of a simple break-in. Perhaps the previous tenants didn't even matter.

Perhaps they *were* digging into lives that were meant to be left alone.

This was a simple stalker. A case for sure, but nothing so complex.

But if they could prevent a mad man from stalking an innocent women, then all the better.

* * * * *

Joe found Irene in her armchair by the fireplace. Her legs were pulled up to her chest, face buried in her knees. Her breathing was steady and for a moment he thought she might actually have fallen asleep.

Suddenly, she spoke. "You've come with good news?"

There were red marks on her cheeks in the shape of her trousers' fabric.

"I may have a break in this case and a suspect for us."

Irene sprang from her seat like a loaded coil. "Amazing news, Doctor!"

Chapter V

Confronting the (Probable) Culprit

As Irene parked on the street in front of Scotland Yard, she heard Joe let out a sigh.

Her friend had been excited at the possible resolution to this mystery, but since their drive downtown, he'd been rather thoughtful. Not unusual for Joe, but he was usually chattier on the hunt.

"You should be proud of yourself, Joe," Irene attempted to cheer him up. "You got our suspect."

He let out a huff of a laugh. "I may have sacrificed a good conversation with Sarah to get that information."

"Oh, it's Sarah. Don't you worry. She is madly in love with you. She will forget all about it the next time you smile at her."

"My smile can do all that?"

"Objectively, yes." She shot him a sly grin.

He drew his eyebrows together and looked out the window.

"Sarah told you she understands that you were on a case. Whether those words were all true or not doesn't matter now. We're here, ready to wrap this up."

Evidently, empathy was not her strong suit. However, she almost always could pull her partner from his dreary mood, whether by force or humour.

Joe looked at her again, regarding her to a point where she quirked an eyebrow.

His gaze looked distant, like a thousand new thoughts burst like a kaleidoscope of butterflies, taking flight.

He finally nodded. "You're right. I am here with you and we are working on something important."

"Not as important as I would've liked. But alas! At least it is something!"

Inside, Scotland Yard was buzzing with activity. A dozen new recruits stood in the lobby, addressed by a tired-looking officer.

As she passed them, Irene gave the rookies a quick once-over. A handful of them would surely pass the tests, but there was one with a shaky leg, and several others trying to hide the fact that they were either hungover or still drunk from the previous night. She frowned. This was the future of Scotland Yard?

"Shame," she muttered.

"What?"

She shook her head at Joe as they entered the main precinct. As they beelined for Lestrade's office, Thom beat them to it and flagged them down.

"Holmes," he called, weaving through the desks and lowering his voice as he approached. "Do you have that file for me?"

"What file?"

The inspector looked at Joe for support, then back to Irene. "The one about the break-ins."

"Ah, of course." Irene remembered but couldn't quite place where she'd put it. "We do not have it with us. We're still in the middle of the case."

Thom raised a brow. "There was an actual case in there?"

"There was, in fact. Now, unless you have time to speak to us about someone, we shall be on our way."

"I don't. I'm in the middle of a case myself."

Irene snorted. "Do let us know if you require help."

The DI pursed his lip. "I certainly won't. Good luck with yours though."

"Likewise," Irene said before continuing toward Eddy's office.

Behind her, Joe sighed. "I can never tell if you are becoming better friends with Gregory or worse enemies."

"Both at the same time."

She rapped hard on the glass door of her oldest friend's workspace, causing Joe to cringe.

"You are going to shatter that door one day."

"If Scotland Yard didn't put strong enough glass to withstand my fist, then that is their own fault."

Eddy looked up from his desk and waved them in..

"Much better," Irene said, gesturing to his mouth, which was now clean-shaven. All remnants of the ludicrous attempt at growing facial hair gone.

"Yes, well, everyone seemed to have a problem with it," he said. "Do you have that file for Thom?"

"Like I told him, we are in the middle of the case and require it."

Eddy gave his usual long-suffering sigh and pinched the bridge of his nose. "*Of course* you found a case."

Irene sat down and leaned on the pile of papers on his desk, steepling her fingers.

"I need you to pull a file of a man that you arrested a while ago. His name is Matthew Stroll."

"Why?"

"Because I require it."

Joe put his hand gently on her shoulder and she took a breath. She was learning that whenever he executed such a gesture, he was intervening before their current situation turned sour.

Her partner took over. "There is a woman in the house that was broken into last night who used to see a man with anger issues. He was quite aggressive and used to stalk her. I managed to secure his name and we think this may be our culprit."

Eddy gestured to Joe, then looked pointedly at Irene. "That, good lady, is how you explain yourself and get what you want."

Irene scoffed again. "I get what I want regardless, Eddy."

The DI stood. "And make many enemies along the way, to be sure. Give me a moment. I will go find the file."

He left the office and Joe laughed, settling into the seat beside her. "You'll find, one day, that you catch more flies with honey than with vinegar."

"Yes, but then you attract insects that you don't want."

Joe reached over to pat her hand. "Quite right."

A few moments later, Eddy returned with the file.

Irene grabbed it immediately. The inspector rolled his eyes as Joe shrugged. She paid them no mind, instead flipping through the notes, half of which was a simple profile. Matthew Stroll had been arrested a few times for public disturbance and threatening an officer while drunk.

Otherwise, he was as clean.

She read the pages again, as if some new information would appear. When none came, she spun to Eddy.

"This is it?"

"He was hardly a hardened criminal."

"You didn't even record his shoe size!" Irene tossed the file on the desk. "Oh, Eddy. You make my job so difficult sometimes."

"I make *your* job difficult?"

Joe placed both hands on Irene's shoulders and gently turned her toward the door. "Alright. We are going to leave before smoke starts coming out of the poor man's ears."

"Of course, we are leaving. There is nothing more for us here."

Joe ushered them out. "Good day, Lestrade."

They wove back through the desks, and past the group of recruits, now all swaying with tiredness as the senior officer droned on about the precinct's history.

The pair climbed into the Vauxhall and Joe shifted in his seat to look at his friend.

"If I may be so bold."

"You may be as bold as you like around me Joe, you know that."

"Alright then." He cleared his throat. "You seem irritated at this case, even though you desperately wanted it."

Irene paused with the key in the ignition. "I did want a case. But to have this whole mess turn out to simply be a man obsessed with a woman is disappointing."

"To stop a man from harassing a poor woman is not disappointing."

"You know what I mean."

"Luckily, I do. But others might not."

She raised a brow at him and gestured around the car. "We are the only ones here."

"I know," he sighed, then tried again, but gave up and slumped in his seat.

"I simply thought that our first case after such a long winter would be... Oh, I don't know." Irene slapped the steering wheel.

"Spies and scandals? Mayhem and madness?"

This earned him a tired laugh. "Something along those lines, yes."

"I think London is getting past that, what with everything settling down."

"Perhaps you're right."

Irene started the engine and pulled away from the kerb.

London had changed since the war, and perhaps after several years of dodging bombs and helping Scotland Yard, everything was calming. There had to be more, though. With its rich history, London simply couldn't turn into a quiet country town without at least some underlying scandal or two.

Joe shifted in the seat, adjusting his tall frame. "What now? Do we visit this man? Was there even a permanent address in the file?"

"There was. But first, I will speak to Maria to see what she knows about him. If he is, in fact, our culprit, we may go ourselves to confront him, or I may call Eddy."

"If we are to confront anyone with a violent attitude, I would prefer to do it with the backup of Scotland Yard."

"As would I in most cases."

"Why not all?"

A sly smile spread cross Irene's lips. She glanced at Joe as the car stopped at a red light. "Because Scotland Yard has rules to follow when confronting a criminal."

* * * * *

After dropping Joe off at Baker Street, Irene headed over to Sarah's house. She had no way of knowing if Maria was home – well, she could've deducted it, but she had no time for that currently. So, she knocked on the door and waited.

Thankfully, Maria opened the door. But not-so-thankfully, the woman dismissed Irene immediately.

"Sarah's not here. She'll be back later tonight."

"Actually, I came to see you." Irene stepped into the house without waiting for a proper invitation. "You should really peer through the blinds or at least ask who is out there before you open the door. Especially with this man on the loose."

She should've bit her tongue, but the words tumbled out before she could think about them.

Maria set her wide shoulders but Irene held up her hand, halting whatever she was going to say.

"I truly apologize. I did not come here to chastise you. The opposite, in fact."

The woman folded her arms across, huffing. "Well, you should make it quick. I was on my way to the grocer. I go every week at this time as he holds flour aside for me."

Irene balked at the demand but kept the snark to herself.

"If we may sit." She suggested instead, shrugging off her jacket and gloves. "This conversation would be better suited over a cup of tea."

Maria dropped her arms to her side. "Now you are scaring me."

"Oh no. It's not scary. I just require some information on Matthew Stroll and find it's better to converse in comfort."

Five minutes later, Irene sat across from Sarah's friend in the living room, a cup of tea in front of them both.

Maria fiddled with her dress. "Sarah said you might come asking about him. I had thought that maybe it was him scaring us at first."

"And you don't think that anymore?"

"He was never violent like that."

"Did he ever lay hands on you?"

"No. If anything, he treated me like a trophy or prize."

"Until he became obsessed with you."

Maria nodded and shifted on the couch. The way she looked to the door and tried to sit as still as possible told Irene she wanted this conversation to end.

"Have you seen him since moving here?"

Maria shifted in her seat again. Irene leaned forward, hoping to comfort the woman as best she could.

"It is just you and I. And I assure you, I will keep everything confidential, if you wish. Even from Scotland Yard."

"He did find us," the lady admitted. "The night we went dancing. He knows we live here."

"And have you told him to leave you alone?"

She shook her head, seemingly embarrassed. "As bold as I have been to you, I don't think I could summon the courage to tell this man off, if I may admit that."

Irene watched her for a moment as frustration brewed inside. She'd noticed not only a crime shift in London since the war ended, but also a social shift. Women were back to either being housewives or to menial jobs instead of running the country as they had done while the men were away. And it seemed like their personalities and strength had been quashed as well.

"What did you do during the war, Maria?"

"I worked in the steel factory."

"You made bombs."

"That's correct, but what does that–"

Irene stood to pace, ready to lecture. "You've handled something that could level a building, did jobs that even men cannot handle, and you have the backup of a strong group of women here. Yet, you allow this man to frighten you? We all made it through the war as strong, brave women, and now that these *men* are back, it's like we've forgotten what we're capable of. If you don't want him pursuing you, then tell him as such. Take your girlfriends. Take me and I will aid you. Hell, I'll even tell him off for you."

At first, all Maria did was stare wide-eyed. "Will it be that easy?"

"We will make it that easy."

Something out the front window caught Maria's attention. She paled and her hands tightened on her dress.

Irene didn't have to look to know the man was standing on the pavement. What luck.

"You said you visit the grocers every week at the exact same time, correct? How long have you been doing that? Long enough, I suspect, for him to figure out that particular schedule."

The stunned woman covered her mouth.

"Oh my. I believe you're right."

"Of course I am." Irene turned to the window, but the road outside was empty.

"He just left."

"He won't be far. Especially if you are still in the house. I must go out and observe him, just quickly. I will know instantly if he is our culprit. You may come with me, if you like, and speak with him while I am present. Or, you may sit in here and not say a word. The choice is completely yours; I will not fault you for either."

Maria stood, but stayed in the sitting room. "I think... I think I will go talk to him. Will you come with me?"

Again, Irene bit her tongue. Is that not what she had told the woman? She needed to observe him, so she was going out there whether this lady was or not. Instead of saying all of this, though, she nodded.

"Of course."

They left the house and Irene spotted the man on his way back to do another pass-by.

As soon as she saw him, her shoulders slumped. This was not their culprit. His feet were too small. Pace too quick.

But Matthew Stroll noticed her, then saw Maria behind on the step. He stopped. Irene moved back beside Maria, in case he got any ideas. He didn't seem like the type to strike out, but men could be unpredictable.

"Maria," he said, voice cracking.

"You..." The woman started, then looked to Irene, who nodded in encouragement. "You need to leave me alone."

"I just wanted to talk."

"No." Maria's voice grew stronger with every word. "You and I are through. I want to be left alone."

He moved forward, and so did Irene.

"But, Maria, my sweetheart. I love you. I just want you back." He shuffled forward.

A tremor shuddered her shoulders and Irene stiffened. Even if this man hadn't hit her, he had been physical somehow, and her body was revolting.

After the disappointment of this case, and now the adrenaline kicking in because there was still a suspect at large, she needed an outlet for her raging emotions.

"Sir," Irene snapped from behind Maria's shoulder. "You've been asked to leave."

"And you might be?"

"I'm the one you're going to deal with if you don't heed our warnings."

"This is between me and Maria."

"And yet, I am here as well. Leave before I make you."

"Are these the types of people you're now friends with? Cheeky broads like this? It's not you, Maria–"

"Please leave!" Maria screeched.

Matthew jerked back, startled. His eyes darkened and he bunched his shoulders, turning angry.

"I will not."

It was time for Irene to intervene. She cut in front of Maria, separating the two.

"Sir, you are a waste of space and oxygen. Depart at once or I will have those constables over there drag you away. And should you come back, you will end up in the basement floorboards of one of these houses and no one will hear from you again."

The jilted man looked at his former lover, who remained still, then he turned his gaze back to Irene.

She raised an eyebrow and folded her arms across her chest.

"Call my bluff, if you dare."

For a brief moment, she thought he might come at her. Instead,

Matthew stepped away and adjusted his coat.

"Clearly there are issues you need to work through and I simply don't have time to deal with that. Nor time to deal with your friend here. Good day."

He pivoted and walked away.

Irene took one last look at him, but not one part matched the man she saw that evening on the street, nor the clues inside the house.

She sighed, but felt slightly elated. This was not the man, but that meant the case was still open. Which meant more sleuthing and intrigue.

Small hands clutched her arm, startling her.

"I think he is actually gone! I can't believe it."

Irene leaned away, stiffening under Maria's touch. "Yes, well. He might not be gone for good, but it'll be a while before he returns, and if he does, you may deal with him, or ring me and I will come over."

"Thank you. Please, come inside and we can finish our tea."

"Oh, I really must be going now–"

"Oh please! The others will be home soon and I must tell them the tale."

Ten minutes later, Irene sat with a fresh cuppa and a plate of biscuits. She'd tried to take up the chair but ended up nestled between Sarah and her friend Jenny instead.

Maria told them of the interaction and made Irene out to be

such a hero. All the women looked at her with awe, it almost made her mad at their change of heart. Only a few days ago they held their noses up and scoffed at her. They didn't even want her to come with them dancing.

"How are you so bold?" Jenny asked.

Irene nabbed another biscuit. "I am more skilled and more intelligent than almost all the men I meet, so I suppose that helps. Also, I have nothing to lose if a man doesn't like me. I have nothing to lose if no one likes me."

"But what about the persistent ones? Those who simply don't take no for an answer?"

"If they do not listen to your words, then you either seek out a constable or detective inspector. I have faith in two such DIs; I shall leave their cards. But if you're willing, I would also be happy to teach you all some basic self-defence. You don't need to be stronger than your opponent, just quicker and be able to land a blow that will send him on his way."

The ladies started to chatter and Irene straightened with pride. This kind of bonding, she could definitely do. While there was enjoyment in shopping and drinking tea, and limited gossiping, being in the company of women who wanted to learn the same skills as her was even more exciting.

"We shall set the time once this case is put to bed and I will show you my tricks. Now, if you'll excuse me, I must get going as this case has become more complex."

Sarah walked her out to the pavement.

"What are you doing now with the case?" she asked. The woman had always expressed interest in Irene and Joe's work, mostly due to her worries about Joe's safety.

"We have a former soldier to speak with. It's quite convoluted, but he should shed some light on a few things within the case. Joe is meeting me there. It helps to have someone who also went through the war. Even if they have nothing in common, there is a kinship formed."

Sarah nodded and looked down at the pavement as the wind picked up. "Joe doesn't speak much about his time on the frontlines. I'm not even sure what he did. He confirmed he didn't fly planes or drive tanks, but he barely even mentions much else. Has he spoken to you about anything?"

Irene was going to answer, but stopped herself mid-breath. Joe shared many war experiences with her, it was true. But, if Sarah were to find out, it would hurt her, or tinge her feelings towards him with a sour aftertaste.

For the umpteenth time in the past few days, Irene bit her tongue.

"He has not spoken much to me about it either," she lied. "Do not fret."

She was learning. Her words seemed to calm Sarah immensely. "Okay. Thank you, Irene."

* * * * *

Irene met Joe on Buchanan Street and he looked just as tired as she felt.

"How did you get on with Maria?" he asked.

"Oh excellent. The man showed up outside the house. I confronted him and he scampered away. He was, however, not our culprit. So, we will have to put our whole selves into this case again."

Joe stopped walking. "You confronted him?"

"He was hardly a danger to me. I told him to leave Maria alone and he ran like a dog with its tail between its legs. He shouldn't be a bother anymore."

"Oh Irene..."

"Oh Joe," she mocked. "Let's continue. Also, I have a question."

"Dear Heavens," he said but caught up to her quickly. "Whenever you tell me you have a question, it always ends up being one I am never prepared for."

"Why have you not spoken to Sarah about the war? Surely she has noticed your scar? Or other scars you may have on your body."

His cheeks reddened. "Well, she hasn't seen much of my body, actually. Or, well... I'm not sure how much she's noticed."

"Oh." Irene shrugged. "I do not know how such intimate

things tend to work for each individual person. I had only assumed."

"Of course," Joe stammered. "Also, she doesn't need to hear such horrific things."

"Hm."

Irene paused, brow furrowing. She turned to Joe, hands on her hips as she discovered something new about their friendship.

"I'm starting to see now that it's not just me that separates myself from these women. You treat me differently than how you treat them."

Her partner stared off for a moment, perhaps coming to the same realization himself. He attempted to speak a few times, but no sound came out. Finally, he found his words, his expression softening.

"It hasn't been on purpose, by any means. And it's certainly not because I don't see you as a woman. I suppose, it's because you and I are friends. Best friends, should that be allowed. And there are certain things that apply to our cases that must be shared. So, of course I would tell you such things."

Irene felt her brow pull together even tighter. "But shouldn't you also tell those things to the woman you intend to marry and spend the rest of your life with? Unless you intend stay at Baker Street. But, that sounds unconventional and silly even to me. Though, I wouldn't quite object. As long as–"

"Irene." Joe clutched her shoulders gently, but she felt the strain under his grip. His cheeks were red all the way back to his ears and his chest rose and fell in quick succession. "I would prefer to talk about it either after this case or when we're back at home."

She nodded, immediately agreeing. Her friend appeared on the edge of one of his panic-induced episodes. He hadn't had one in so long, and Irene would be damned if she was the cause of one now.

Joe instantly relaxed, unclenching his jaw and softening the grip on her shoulders. "Thank you."

"Would you like to walk around the block before speaking with the soldier?"

He took a few deep breaths. "No. Thank you. I believe I am okay."

"Excellent."

As they started down the pavement again, though, she linked her arm through his in an attempt to keep him calm, should any of panicked thoughts linger. She was still unsure what caused this episode specifically, but noted that his jaw clenched at mention of leaving Baker Street.

Her face pinched. Emotions were difficult at the best of times, and when they were skewed by a brain that could be triggered so unexpectedly, it made for figuring out other humans very difficult.

Chapter VI

A Soldier's Unfortunate Tale

Even though Joe appeared calm as they walked down the street, worry flooded his mind. He didn't quite know why Irene speaking about his future upset him so. He had always been nervous about big changes in his life, but currently, he felt like he was in a natural progression for once.

And he certainly couldn't ignore her statement about individual intimacy. His cheeks warmed anew. Now was not the time for reflecting on that.

Irene's arm in his made it easier for him to draw breath. By the time they reached their destination, he was prepared for the interview.

The building they arrived at was surprisingly coated in fresh paint. The bright white gleamed even though the sun struggled through the clouds.

The pair had the option to take the lift or the stairs. Standing in the small lobby at the gate for a moment, neither one of them was willing to call the box.

"Shall we take the stairs?" Irene offered.

"We shall."

While the outside of the apartment building was shining new, the interior had yet to be updated. And the last time they were on a lift they'd clung to each other for dear life, and they were trying to avoid the memory of that event.

They found the flat easily enough and Irene gave a sharp knock on the door.

The door opened only a few inches and a middle-aged man peered out.

"Hubert Harriott? My name is Irene Holmes and this is my partner Dr. Watson. We're private detectives and were hoping to ask you a few questions regarding your sister and her friends."

* * * * *

Captain Hubert Harriott was suspicious at first, but he'd let them in.

The flat was dark and sad, just like the man in front of them. Medals sat in a box at the end of a cluttered counter. He hadn't offered them tea, and Irene didn't even spot a kettle anywhere.

Sat at his table, they'd told him briefly about the break-in and that they feared someone is else was in danger.

"What did you want to know about June?" he said, gruff voice matching his husky body and scruffy beard. "I don't like speaking about her much, but… If this helps clear up a few things, then I'll provide what's necessary."

"We want to know what happened in the house she was living in with Carrie and Olivia."

He contemplated his words, then heaved a heavy sigh. "I suppose it doesn't matter anymore. June, Olivia and Carrie got that house with my help, because of my rank. They did everything together – worked, shopped, danced, you name it. As soon as the war hit, the government was all over June to join because she'd studied German in school and knew the language and customs. Meanwhile, Olivia had a knack for accents and was quick to think on her feet. And Carrie could do mathematics faster than anyone I've met. The three of them enlisted, and I hardly saw them during their service. June immediately disappeared. Nothing scandalous, but as someone who could speak the language of the enemy, those government folks scooped her up very quickly.

"Carrie went to Bletchley Park for a time, which left Olivia here, conversing with a few officials and listening to recordings. She and I got along very well before I left and I courted her."

"You left to fight," Joe offered.

Harriott nodded. "I was captured not long after I went in. A group of us happened to be travelling together. Stupid move, looking back on it. They came and snatched us up easy enough.

Spent a few months in that camp until we were rescued. Later, I discovered my own sister had found our location. I couldn't have been prouder."

"Was she there in Germany?" Irene asked. "At the rescue?"

The man shook his head. "She was long gone by then. She had been in the country, yes, but once she gave our location, she returned home lest she was discovered."

"Were Carrie and Olivia involved in your rescue?"

"I'm not sure. They kept the details blurry, but I know they did their fair share when it came to other rescues."

"All of you settled back in London when the war ended?"

Hubert nodded again. "The three women were a bit shaken to say the least. About two weeks after they settled back into that house, Carrie was... Well, she was killed in a brutal manner. I'm sure your police friend will have the file, but read it with caution. They never found the killer – or any clues, for that matter. My poor sister got so paranoid in that home that not even Olivia could offer comfort. June rambled on about the man she'd saved us from. Saying she saw him everywhere. She came to live with me for a time, but never slept. The doctor gave her some sleeping aid, which only gave her night terrors. One night, she and Olivia went out dancing. They rang me shaken up when they got home. Someone had been following them. After that, June went missing for two days."

He paused, eyes brimming with tears. "Scotland Yard found

her in a hotel room. She'd taken too much of her sleeping aid and cut her wrists. No note, but they said it was an obvious suicide."

"*They* said?" Irene interjected. "You never saw June after her boldy was found?"

"After their investigation, they sealed her in the coffin. A part of me is glad I never saw her in that state, but another wishes they'd come to me before they nailed her in there."

Joe's stomach was on edge, the story making him feel queasy. He glanced at Irene, waiting for her to urge the man along. But she held back, stoic and still, giving him a moment.

"We had a rough go after that," Harriott continued. "I told Olivia she was more than welcome to stay at my flat until she found somewhere else, no expectations or conditions. But she refused to leave the house. There was something on her mind and would not leave until she saw it through. Then, one day, she rang and told me that she loved me and wished me the best and that she was leaving the city, possibly to America. She left a note too, for her other friends and family."

"Did she know anyone in America?"

"Not that I know of. And she never met any Americans during the war. In fact, she had mentioned a few times in passing that she *never* fancied going over there. But perhaps the whole ordeal changed the girl's mind because she made sure to tell everyone and was quite adamant. She didn't want me at the docks to see her off. Said it would be too painful to wave goodbye to me."

"Curious." Irene sat back on the couch, pondering.

"You think?"

Joe looked between them, trying to figure out what made Irene take note of that particular detail. The only thing he could think of was that, if Olivia had been trained by Bletchley or any other government official, then perhaps her making such a point of leaving was a diversion.

Irene suddenly leaned forward. "Is there anything else you can provide for us?"

Harriot shrugged. "I only have one photograph of the women from when I borrowed a friends camera. Let's see if I can find it."

"That would be lovely. Then we shall leave you alone."

The veteran stepped into a den; they heard him rifle through some papers.

Joe didn't realize how tense he was until Irene's hand gently grasped his wrist.

"This took a very sad turn," he whispered.

"It did, indeed." She kept her voice low as well. "But also a very intriguing one."

Harriott returned, handing them a photograph. Olivia, June and Carrie stood in a line, grasping each other's arm, with big smiles on their pretty faces. They were so similar to Sarah and her friends that it made Joe squirm. He did notice a scar on Olivia's face though, and wondered how she had received it.

"You can keep it." The man's voice cracked. "I'm not sure I can look at it any longer."

Irene nodded and went to tuck it in her purse.

Joe stopped her. "Are you certain, Captain? We would hate to keep a memory from you."

"I am sure."

"If you'd ever like it back, we will leave our card for you to call. We'd be happy to return it." He fished a business card from his pocket. "Thank you for all your help. It is much appreciated."

"I just hope no one else gets hurt. If you folks can prevent that, then this dredging up of old memories will be worth it."

"That is valiant of you, sir. Thank you."

Irene mumbled a thank-you as well and shuffled behind Joe, clearly eager to leave the house.

Joe shook the man's hand again and followed her out.

Once on the pavement, she spoke. "You always know what to say. Which is good, because I never know how to end heavy moments like that."

"I suppose that's what makes us a fine team." He never thought of himself as a particularly good people-person – hence why he'd gone into animal medicine – but compliments from Irene were few and far between, so he gobbled this one up.

"Quite right," she said, then clasped her hands together. "Olivia Bennett is alive and well in London."

"I knew it!" At Irene's sly look, he said, "I mean, I guessed that perhaps she was making too much of a point in saying she was leaving."

She beamed up at him, brown eyes sparkling in the streetlight. "Brilliant deduction, Doctor. That is exactly what I think as well. So, we have two dead women and one who claims to have left London but hasn't."

"How do we find her?"

"That I have not yet figured out yet. It requires pondering. Obviously, if she was trained to be a spy, then she will not be easy to find. However, there are different avenues we can take; I just need to figure out the best one."

"Do you think the man June claimed to have seen is real?"

"I do, and I have a hunch it's our burglar. We need to take another thorough look in as many of those houses as we can. Ring Sarah tonight and ask if we can tear apart her house. Then we shall see about getting into the others. But, for now, back to Baker Street for dinner. Perhaps we will even get a peaceful night's sleep for once."

* * * * *

The telephone shrilled through the quiet flat. Joe leapt from his chair as the second ring flooded the room.

As he stumbled toward the small table to answer the phone, he heard a loud thump from Irene's room, followed by a series of curse words.

"Joe Watson speaking."

"Sorry to wake you, Joe." Lestrade's voice came through slightly muffled and tired. "I'm currently at Sarah James' house. Everyone is unharmed..." Whatever Lestrade said next, Joe didn't hear. His heart thudded and sweat had appeared on his forehead.

Irene had finally emerged, rubbing her shin. She rushed to him, but he waved her down.

"It's Lestrade." He put the phone back to his ear. "Apologies. What happened?"

Irene wiggled next to him and stood on her tiptoes, listening in.

"Someone has thrown a smoke bomb into the house. Everyone is a bit rattled but safe. I've kept them out of the house if the two of you want to pop down here and investigate."

Irene nodded emphatically.

"We shall," Joe said. "Thank you."

He set the receiver down and rubbed his eyes. Beside him, his partner stretched her arms, waking herself some more.

"When we find the culprit, I shall slap him silly for interrupting so much of my sleep."

* * * * *

Irene drove to the house, seemingly fully alert and eager as a bloodhound on the hunt. Joe, however, stifled yawn after yawn.

A large fire engine was parked on the street, a few firemen leaning on the truck, waiting for the all-clear from Lestrade before they departed the scene. A police car was parked beside the familiar Wolseley.

"You deal with the women," Irene said as she pulled up beside Lestrade's car. "But don't linger. I've a hunch this was meant to scare them and see who would respond. As soon as you can, join me inside. I will take a quick look, but I don't not want to start my thorough investigation without you."

Joe immediately went toward the terrified group of women. As soon as Sarah saw him, she ran and flung herself into his arms. A few constables glanced over, and the other women looked they wanted to fling themselves at him as well. Joe's ears warmed in embarrassment.

"It's alright," he soothed her. "You are safe. Why don't you ladies tuck in close to the building while Irene and I look at the house."

"We saw him," Sarah said. "Well, sort of."

Joe released her as if burned. "You did? One moment."

He spun to find Irene about to enter the house and shouted

after her. She scrambled over as fast as she could.

"Sorry, dear," Joe addressed to Sarah, adding a sentiment to ease his urgency of turning from boyfriend to investigator so quickly. "Can you tell us what happened? In as much detail as possible."

His girlfriend hesitated briefly, but Joe had no idea how to reassure her.

Irene stepped forward and placed her hand on Sarah's shoulder in an action so human that Joe turned to look quizzically at her.

"You are safe," she said. "What you tell us may be enough to finally figure out who this man is and make sure he never bothers you again."

This seemed to comfort Sarah immensely. He'd rarely seen Irene act so sympathetic toward someone and thought that perhaps this was a little glimmer of hope that she was learning empathy.

Irene gestured to the other women. "Did they have any stories separate from yours or were they panicking too much to notice anything?"

Joe sighed. And there she was, his Irene, brash and tactless.

Sarah didn't seem to notice – and if she did, didn't seem to mind.

"They would have the same story, I believe. I heard a noise, like a loud bang. There was smoke from the upstairs lavatory and I shouted for everyone to wake up. We all ran downstairs, sure it was a fire. But we smelled no fire and felt no heat. However, someone was walking around upstairs. We thought about running out, but those were our bedrooms up there, with all our possessions. We remembered what you said, Irene. About the things we used to handle during the war and how brave we used to be. Jenny rang Scotland Yard while the rest of us armed ourselves with pots and pans and things to throw. Then we marched back upstairs.

"A man, like the one you described the other night, was stomping around as if looking for something. The smoke still filled the room, but we could see his outline. We started throwing things at him. The heavy pan I had grabbed struck his head and he fell into the lavatory, then climbed back out of the window."

Sarah stopped talking, her breath short and quick, as if she just relived the entire scenario all over again.

Joe stared at her, then at Irene, in awe of how his friend had bolstered this group of women up so much that they confronted a potential madman.

"That was brilliant," Irene said. "Well done to you all! I do have some follow-up questions though. What rooms had he already been in?"

"All but mine," Sarah replied. "He was heading there when we went up the stairs."

"Excellent!" Irene turned in a flourish and gestured to the

small crowd gathered outside their homes to nosey about the situation. "Do you see the man amongst the people here tonight? Often the perpetrator will return to see who he is up against."

Sarah looked amongst the crowd then shook her head. "I don't, I'm sorry."

"Nothing to apologize for. We will search the house now. You all may go into the kitchen and get a cuppa. I have a feeling that what we are looking for will be upstairs. Especially since this man went to such trouble to get himself up there and to chase you from your rooms." She turned to Joe. "You and I will traverse the back garden for any signs that may help us further, then we will search Sarah's bedroom."

Joe was still baffled as to the whole situation, but he looked to his girlfriend. "Is that okay? If we search your room?"

"Of course. Whatever you need to do."

Irene had already taken off toward the house. He followed.

Lestrade stood in the foyer, picking at his fingernail, looking like he needed to sleep for about ten years.

"Eddy, there is something in this house that is important and we are not leaving here until we find it."

"Excellent. Do you require my further assistance?"

"Joe and I are going to investigate the back garden, but once that is clear, and we don't need your assistance in possibly pursuing a criminal, you may instruct everyone except the constables to go home. I want a pair of them here every minute of the day until this man is caught."

"You telling me how to order my men around now?"

"Yes. It is necessary, as they've allowed someone to infiltrate this house for a second time now." She waved away his attitude with her hand. "The women are coming in. They are all shaken and full of adrenaline. See to it that they get a cup of tea and relax while we search the upstairs. Come, Joe. To the garden."

Irene zipped away, the thrill of the mystery fuelling her. Joe stood back with Lestrade for a moment, watching her go.

The DI let out a snort. "I'm not quite sure what just happened."

"You were given a list of orders. In a rather serious tone. Heaven help you if you don't follow through."

"Joe!" Irene called from the garden. "Where are you?"

"Heaven help *you* if you don't get out there," Lestrade quipped back. They exchanged exhausted smiles and Joe continued through the house.

His partner was flat against the ground when he joined her in the back garden. She shone a torch around, stopping in some places before grumbling and hopping to her feet.

"Nothing," she snapped. "Well, a few spots of blood, but no trail to follow."

"Whoever this is, he has a few tricks up his sleeve."

"Then we must have more."

"Back inside, then?"

He turned, knowing she'd want to get a move on with her

investigation, but Irene surprisingly stayed put on the grass. Joe slowly turned back to her.

Usually her questions were about cases, but lately they'd turned to asking about social interactions, and sometimes caught Joe completely off-guard. He had no idea what to expect from her when he met her curious gaze.

"Why did you ask permission to go into Sarah's room? You two have been seeing each other for long enough, I thought you'd have permission already."

Joe breathed a sigh of relief. It could've been worse.

"Because it's someone's private space. You always ask permission."

"Even if you are dating and have most likely seen their room, or at least the items in it, prior?"

"I haven't seen Sarah's room."

"Not at this house, but at her other flat, you must have."

"Well, yes, I have," he stammered. "It's just one of those things, I suppose. It's someone's bedroom. You ask, regardless of your relationship with them."

"Oh."

"Why? Have you been in my room when I am not present?"

Irene shrugged. "Not often. But if I require a book or wish to use your mirror. Your window lets in more natural light than mine does, and sometimes I need it if I try a new lipstick."

"Irene..."

"I do not snoop!"

"That is your literal job!"

"Okay, well I don't *actively* snoop through your things. Do you have that many secrets hidden away?"

Joe slumped his shoulders, realizing that he was in no way offended or embarrassed. "No, I suppose not."

"Besides, you are more than welcome to go into my room should you require any of my books or other items."

"I shall keep that in mind," he said, then a thought occurred to him about an emotion he'd never seen Irene display. "Does nothing embarrass you?"

She genuinely considered his question for a moment, then shrugged. "I am beyond embarrassment when it comes to you, I believe."

"Ah. So, there are no conversations I could have with you that would make you blush?"

A sly smirk spread across her face. "I feel that any conversation that would make *me* blush, would also cause your face to redden, thus you wouldn't approach the subject in the first place."

Joe playfully scowled at her. "Fine, you have me there."

She adjusted her gloves, wrapping up the conversation, as if she'd won a battle. "Now, inside. Let's figure out what this man was looking for."

Irene passed through the entire house and Joe followed her

upstairs to Sarah's room. The small bed was tucked in the corner. A vanity sat against the wall, with a few bags of Sarah's belongings yet to be unpacked.

"Go into the closet and poke around," Irene ordered. "I shall look around the window and door."

Joe stepped into the small closet, pushing aside the two dresses that hung there. Nothing of note stuck out, but he'd learned from a case they'd worked on last year that anything could be hidden anywhere. For example, a secret door at the back of the closet that led them to a dead body. Not that Joe wanted to find a dead body here as well, but anything at this point would be welcome.

He knocked on the wood, moving his knuckle along. At one point, a hollow sound did come through.

He stopped and rapped on the wood again, at that specific spot.

"Irene!" Within seconds, she squeezed into the closet with him.

"Listen," he knocked on the wood again, showing the difference in the sound.

His partner squished closer to him, her elbow jabbing into his stomach and her rose scented curls smothering his face.

"I'm quite capable of seeing what's in there," he said, voice muffled in her hair.

Her fingers immediately went for the wood in front of the

hollow space. She picked away at it then cursed.

"My fingers are not strong enough. You get it, Joe."

She finally moved away and he raised an eyebrow.

"What?" she said. "I am eager."

"I am well aware."

He wedged his fingers into a small slot, prying a wooden piece off the closet.

Irene looked it over quickly, finding nothing of importance, so she tossed it on the ground.

Joe shone the torch into the small space in the wall, lightening up something akin to a brick. He reached in, feeling around, and his fingers fell upon a hardcover book. He wedged it out, dust puffing into the air.

Irene gasped and snatched it from his hands.

At first, she opened it in front of her face, then, as if realising, tilted it so Joe could see as well.

The pages were filled with spaced out names. The first dozen were all blacked out with heavy ink. Irene flipped carefully but quickly, coming to a page with several women's names with different symbols beside each one – a star, a checkmark, a dash...

"A woman's writing?" Joe asked.

Irene nodded. "Using several different types of pens at different times."

Almost all the names had an address and one word after:

DEAD

Irene flipped the page as Joe's heart raced. There had to be at least twenty names on these pages, and more than half of them belonged to deceased women. There was no indication of how they'd gone, though, and no further explanation of why the names were written down. One caught his attention and Irene saw it at the same time:

Carrie Harrison. 12 St. Mary's. DEAD

Irene shot him a quick, worried glance, then kept flipping the pages. "All the names and addresses were written mostly at the same time. Look at the angle and pressure. Then look at the word *dead* on each line – it was written after. Someone is going through this list and either tracking these women or killing them."

She flipped to the last used page. Three other names were written, with a fourth and last one that they both recognized:

Olivia Bennett – ALIVE.

Three London addresses were scribbled underneath, with one stroked out.

Joe tapped the book. "The writing descends into scribbles by the end. As if this person grew more frustrated or mad, as if losing their mind."

"And one name is missing. June Harriott is not in this book."

"Perhaps it was written by another woman after June killed herself?"

"Or this is why she did." Irene closed the book with such force that a puff of dust floating into the air. "This has to be what that man's been searching for. Put the wood back. No one must know that we've found anything."

"Won't that stop this man from breaking into the house?"

"It would, yes, but then it would make him disappear, and we need to figure out who he is first."

Joe put his hand on her shoulder. "Irene, we can't leave Sarah and her friends here again unprotected."

"They were capable enough tonight. Plus, I will have the constables at their door and back garden, even if I need to bribe them myself." She tucked the book into her bag. "We must get home and write all of this out. And we must find Olivia. Come, Joe!"

Irene strode to the door and was down the stairs within seconds, leaving him to stare after her. He felt his heartrate kick up in a familiar excitement. The hunt was truly on.

While this case had an air of danger about it, he realized that even he had been affected by the dull winter.

He shoved the wood back in its place, assuring there were no cracks showing. Out on the street, the Vauxhall started its engine and Joe rushed downstairs and out the front door before Irene drove away.

Chapter VII

A Trip to Parliament

That morning, Irene stared at Joe as they perched in their respective chairs at Baker Street.

"Chin up, Joe. I'm sure Sarah will understand. It was the middle of the night and we were on a case. I stopped into the kitchen and gave them a simple explanation, so I'm sure your not saying goodbye or even acknowledging them is fine."

Joe groaned.

She scrunched her face. "Did that not help? I thought it would. Do you want one of these biscuits?"

She grabbed a jam-filled sweet from the plate on the table, but Joe shook his head.

"No, thank you. I shall try ringing her again after Mrs. Grouper's visit."

Irene set the cookie back on the plate. She knew Joe's lament wasn't completely over, but she had no other comfort to offer while they waited for their guest to arrive.

Henriette Grouper's timing couldn't have been better when she'd rung and said she would be in the city today. Irene immediately invited her to Baker Street, hoping she could provide some insight to the book of names as the young woman had worked at Bletchley in their decoding program. The three of them became friends since the two investigators helped her with a stalker on their second case together last year.

As if on cue, the front bell rang and, as per usual, Miss Hudson hurried to answer.

Half an hour later, Irene and Henriette sat on the couch, the book between them. The woman had gone through it few times when she finally shook her head.

"I only recognize two of these names. And only in passing. But they definitely worked at Bletchley. There were women who were sent undercover, as often they could slip in and out to gather information that men couldn't. It must have been difficult for them. I did my work from the relative safety of London. I can't imagine being behind enemy lines."

A baby giggle interrupted them. On the other side of the room, Joe sat in his chair with Henriette's two-year-old daughter Maggie on his lap. He bounced her up and down, babbling away in silly baby talk. The little one's plump cheeks were squished in a smile. Meanwhile, Isla danced at his feet, trying to sniff every inch of the equally small creature.

The light outside the window caught Maggie's attention. Joe stood up, taking her to the glass. She banged her little hand, cooing at the activity in the street below.

Irene felt a smile stretch across her face. Her friend was terribly happy playing with this baby; she hoped it kept him cheery the rest of the day.

Beside her, Henriette chuckled. "Looks like your man is having a good time. Will you be having one of your own soon? Or are you not quite ready to put down the magnifying glass?"

"Oh, I don't know if I'll ever be ready for a task as big as that one."

"Should your time come, you'll be ready." She nodded to Joe, still in his own little world. "He certainly is."

Worry stirred in Irene that made her stomach swirl as if someone whisked it with a spoon. She attempted to shake it off so she could get back to the case. Whether Henriette noticed her unease, or simply wanted to continue, she didn't know, but tapped the book nevertheless.

"Most of these names are probably aliases anyway, unless whoever wrote this book knew them. All the original names and whatever projects they worked on would be kept in the archives. But, unless you know someone in the government, access to those are off limits."

Irene laughed. "Funny enough, I do know someone in the government."

"I thought you might," Henriette laughed. "I'm sure I don't have to tell you, but be careful with this one. It's a very slippery slope."

Irene nodded in agreement.

"Also, you and your doctor are more than welcome to come out to visit us, should you need a weekend away from the city. We have plenty of room. Or if you want practice for when you decide to have one of your own."

Irene stuck out her hand as they stood. "You have been most helpful, Henriette."

The woman bypassed the handshake and pulled her friend into a hug. "Thank you again for everything you and Joe did for us."

"It was simply part of the job. And I gained a friend."

"You certainly did."

Henriette wandered over and took her child from Joe as Irene watched on. A friend, indeed. She felt like she was collecting them like a magpie and shiny stones. But it was a good thing. Helpful friends like Henriette, that could hold a conversation with Irene, were certainly welcome in her life.

The woman bid them both a goodbye, waving Maggie's little hand.

Joe and Irene watched from the window as Henriette and her baby climbed into their automobile.

"Was she helpful at all? I admit, I was not paying an ounce of attention."

"She was, yes. You seemed to enjoy yourself."

Joe turned to her, leaning back on her desk. "I helped raise my younger sisters. Babies are fun. But they are more fun when they have parents you can hand them back to."

Irene grabbed the plate of biscuits to take to the counter, nabbing the last one. "Unless they are your own children, I assume?"

He followed, scooping the tray with the mugs. "Well, then I'd probably feel different about them of course.

"Has Sarah mentioned children at all?"

Joe stiffened ever so slightly. "Yes, but she knows we must be married first."

"My father wasn't married."

Joe put his arm around her shoulder and squeezed. "That is true, but I wouldn't call your life typical."

"I will admit, and this mustn't *ever* get to Miss Hudson, but that baby was rather adorable."

Joe's eyes lit up and a mischievous smile spread across his face. "Did you just give me blackmail ammunition, Irene Holmes?"

"Oh, Joe," she patted his cheek. "That is not a battle you will win."

"It's not a battle I thought I'd ever be waging, but imagine the tizzy it would put Miss Hudson in if she knew were even *thinking* about babies."

Irene grabbed her hat and gloves. "I wouldn't stray too far down that road, Joe. Imagine if Miss Hudson knew that you and Sarah had been speaking about houses and moving away? Imagine the heartbreak!"

Joe regarded her with a smirk. "You have got me there, I admit. Where are you off to?"

"To speak to Mr. Cullens." She tugged on her jacket, then shoved the book in her bag. "Henriette suggested I speak with him as he might know these names and would shed some light on this mystery."

"That poor man. You should put him out of his misery by either telling him to stay away or accepting his offers."

"Let me get what I need out of him, then I shall decide what to do."

"No, Irene that's not..."

He trailed off as she scampered out of the flat.

* * * * *

Mr. Basil Cullens worked in one of the wings to the side of the Parliament building. Irene entered through a large door and headed straight to the receptionist desk.

She made sure her curls were tucked in place and put an extra bounce in her step. Her plan was simple: coerce Mr. Cullens into giving her information. Of course, he'd be reluctant, but hopefully his feelings for her would soften him up.

Was it a bit cruel? Yes. But lives were at stake.

The secretary looked up. "Can I help you, miss?"

"I'm here to see Mr. Basil Cullens, please."

"Do you have an appointment?"

Irene leaned on the desk. "I don't, but I'm Irene Holmes. I just need him for a quick moment."

A man approached the desk. "Irene Holmes, you say?"

Irene gave him a quick once-over. Typical government man. Pressed suit, no pets, heavy smoker.

"Yes."

"I know who you are. Cullens will be glad to see you. He's been trying to get a hold of you."

The tall man led her down the long hallway. She took every opportunity to look into each room as she passed. Most of them were standard offices, full of dusty books; all the secrets probably tucked away on other levels of the building.

Cullens' office was down one of the side corridors. These offices were smaller, but still separate from the main hub of the rest of the workers. Perhaps she did need to make more use of her suitor; keep him around as a contact. That meant a dinner or two.

Irene tucked her dismay away as they reached his door. The man gave a sharp rap on the wood.

"Yes?" Cullens' voice was a sharp bark of a sound and a part of it impressed Irene. The man opened the door and stuck his head in.

"An Irene Holmes for you."

"Oh!" The rough voice perked up instantly.

Irene felt the tiniest bit of guilt, but she shook it away quick. Only wit and cunning were of use at that moment. And perhaps some charm.

The man held the door open for her and she stepped inside the small office.

Cullens stood upon her entrance, a broad smile on his square face. His dark hair was slicked back, his suit freshly pressed. The man was handsome, Irene would admit. But she wouldn't let that break her focus.

He gestured for her to sit across from him.

Once perched in front of his desk, she spoke.

"I actually have some names I wanted to run by you to see if they triggered anything in your memory. Or if you had access to a database for them."

He tried his best to hide his expression, but his jaw tightened and his eyebrows fell. "Ah, so you are here on business, then."

"If we were conversing for pleasure, we would not be sitting in your office."

"Indeed," he said, leaning forward. "And will we ever get to speak for pleasure?"

Irene cringed inwardly. This was the exact conversation she

was hoping to avoid.

"Perhaps when I am finished this case. I know you've been trying to reach me."

"Trying to reach you? I've all but showed up on your doorstep."

"Yes, well…" She picked some fluff from her trousers. "I am here now about a case, then we may discuss the whole greenhouse you've sent."

He seemed satisfied enough and spoke as he straightened a pen on his desk. "What names were you looking into, and where did you find them?"

She produced the book, but kept it in her grasp as she showed him, noting any changes in his expression. He seemed curious, but no recognition yet.

"That looks well loved. Where did you get it from?"

"That does not matter. The names–"

"It does, however, as the names may be connected to the place you discovered the book."

Irene shook her head. "I will disclose the location if you recognize any of the names."

Mr. Cullens sighed and straightened the pen again. He was agitated.

Irene wasn't trying to be difficult on purpose, but a book full of women's names seemed suspicious enough. She felt protective of them even though they were complete strangers to her.

She read out a few names, keeping a close watch for any signs of recognition. After a few names, the man sighed.

"It would make matters easier if I were to see the names on this list."

She ignored his statement and read the next name, "Carrie Harrison."

Cullens stiffened ever so slightly, giving Irene her answer.

"You know this woman?"

He shook his head and overdid the sigh. "No. Just like I don't know the rest of them. May I please know where you found the book?"

She ignored his question. "June Harriott."

He licked his lips, glancing over at his pen and pad, as if wanting to write a note.

"You know that one as well."

"I do not."

"You do."

"Irene, you must trust me a little. You came to me after all."

She folded her arms across her chest. "I trust you in as much as I trust your knowledge of things."

"If you had let me take you to dinner, I bet you would trust me a lot more."

"Well, that is not the current case, is it?"

Cullens sat back. "Why did you ignore me all those times?"

Clear deflection – a move that almost got her as she was keen on jumping to the defence. But she also was here to finish a job.

As smart as Mr. Cullens was, she was smarter.

"We are moving away from the task at hand."

"Tell me why you won't let me take you to dinner"

"Stop deflecting. I did not accept a dinner invitation because I do not want dinner."

"With me?"

"With anyone."

"Does Dr. Watson still live with you?"

Her eyes narrowed. "Couldn't you find that information out on your own?"

"Irene, you are becoming difficult," he said, with an angered sigh.

She stared at him and clenched her jaw. She closed the book carefully and placed both hands on the cover, sitting as prim and proper as she could. Her anger was rising and Joe was not here to calm her. In his absence, she tried to imagine his hand on her shoulder, reminding her to remain civil.

"Agent Cullens," Irene drawled out, calm and carefully. "I asked you if you could identify any names in this book. You said no, but your body language tells a different story. If you would please–"

"I will answer–"

"I am speaking, sir," she snapped. "Now, do you, or do you

not recognize any names in this book?"

Cullens stared at her, seemingly weighing his options. His ears were turning red, and he hid his fists under the table.

"I do. But I cannot tell you where, for I don't know the full details myself."

"So, they are important women?"

"I believe so, yes."

Irene stayed stoic and seemingly in control, but her fingers twitched. She was dying to know every detail.

"I know they were spies working on various projects. Do you know the names of the projects?"

The agent's face stayed red, his shoulders stiff, but his words kept their calm. "It would not make a difference to you if I did because you do not have access to those files."

"You could go get the files and we could look over them together," she urged, a bit desperately. "Or you could tell me the names."

"Fine. Project Schoolbell and Project Fairytale. Are you happy? They mean nothing to you. The operations are over and there is nothing you can do with those names. Now, I have told you what I know. Give me the damn book."

To her surprise, he'd spoken the truth about the operation names. There was no tell she found to say he lied, and his mounting frustration caused him to slip up.

He was correct, however, in that knowing those names

wouldn't get her very far unless she got her hands on the documents.

Mr. Cullens straightened his pen yet again. "I highly suggest you cease this case, whatever it may be. Or turn the information over to us."

Irene let out a sharp bark of laughter that startled him. "This is my case. I will see it through."

"And if you are in over your head?"

"I live in the depths over my head." She stood up, finished with the conversation. Agent Cullens wasn't going to give her any information. Not without some serious pressure, which she didn't want to give in the middle of a government building. Nor a date, which she didn't want either.

He stood as well, but there was a particular look in his eye, like he'd enjoyed the small bit of fight she'd put up. It made her feel uneasy. So, she dragged her mind back to the case as a new thought came to her. Perhaps she could coerce him into bringing the archived files to this office? He'd be reading over her shoulder, but at least she'd get the information she'd need.

Currently, Cullens was on guard though, and she'd have to treat the matter delicately. Which meant softening her approach.

Irene relaxed her shoulders as much as possible and plastered on a smile.

"Mr. Cullens," she began, voice saccharine sweet. "Perhaps I have been too quick to judge and have been putting up a wall between us. I did not mean to anger you today; I am simply trying to do my job and prove to everyone that I am still useful."

His eyes narrowed in suspicion, but he kept listening.

She gazed downward, playing coy. "You have been nothing but lovely and persistent."

"You're right, I have," the man said, still watching her warily.

She batted her eyelashes up at him and gave her head a small shake, assuring her curls cascaded across her shoulders. Cullens's demeanour changed; a smirk graced his lips.

"I see now that all you've wanted is to take me to dinner." She stroked the collar of his jacket in a move she'd seen Sarah do to Joe that seemed to make him weak in the knees.

The agent inched closer and she tried not to step back. His face was close enough that Irene could smell the expensive pomade in his hair.

"I would still like to take you to dinner, despite that little quarrel we had. Hopefully we won't have one again."

She attempted not to react to the veiled threat. Instead, she smiled sweetly. "I hope not. But there is one thing and then we can put this silly mess to bed and move on with us. What if we went through the files together? You could get them and we could read them, side by side."

She trailed her hand down his arm, intertwining her fingers with his. "Perhaps we can stir up some chemistry before we even go on that date."

The words tasted like ash in her mouth. She knew the exact grimace Joe would make when she told him this story. But her tricks seemed to work.

Some men were so simple.

"Fine. Wait here. And we look only at what I show you."

"Deal." She threw in a wink for good measure.

Cullens gave her a curious but pleased look, his ears red from a different feeling, no doubt, and he left the room. Irene settled in the chair and waited. He would be cautious with what he showed her, but if that little charade worked, perhaps similar tactics would as well.

Within ten minutes, he returned with two boxes, setting them on the desk. Irene immediately went for them, but the agent kept his hands on the lids.

"I will pull out what is relevant."

She wanted to talk back, but instead sat prim and proper and nodded.

He pulled out two folders, then settled beside her.

"The women from that book are all dead, unfortunately. So there isn't much to tell. Some of them died during bombings, some were terminated by the enemy. A few took their own lives."

"You and your people couldn't do anything to help them once they returned from the war?" Irene asked.

"Most of them refused help. They distrusted everyone. Shame, because we could've used a lot of the women in our offices today."

She snorted. "You'd stick them with secretary duty, no doubt."

Cullens glared. "Not all women were demoted."

"But most were displaced."

"I am not going to argue politics with you. Now, I'm not sure what more you want to know."

Everything.

There were more files in there that she knew held information and addresses for the women who were still alive, according to the book. She knew Cullens wouldn't let her have free reign to read, so she needed to either get him or the files out of the room.

She cleared her throat. "Is there a file on Olivia Bennet in there?"

Cullens looked through the box and nodded. "There is. It says she is alive but out of the country. No address."

His voice hitched and the difference was so subtle that Irene almost missed it.

A lie?

Was there, in fact, an address for Miss Bennet? She cleared her throat again, with a little more force.

"What about June Harriott? Does it say her whereabouts?"

He flipped through the files. "It says she was found dead. Scotland Yard ruled it a suicide."

"Would your people have taken over the investigation?"

"There was no investigation."

"Not even with all of her importance?"

"There was barely money for weapons, let alone an investigation of a woman who, quite clearly, killed herself."

Irene cleared her throat for a third time, accompanied the action with a small cough.

Cullens finally took notice.

"Are you okay?"

"Oh yes. The air is just so very dry in here." She coughed again for good measure. "And I suppose it's almost tea time and my body simply wants a nibble."

She glanced at him, eyes big, and she tried her best to make the pleading face Isla did when she wanted Joe's sandwich.

Cullens sighed, then gently touched her cheek. "I do have a weakness for a pretty face, I will admit. What if I brought us some tea?"

She grasped his arm in feigned excitement. "That would actually be so lovely."

He stood, but looked between the boxes and her. Irene held her hands up.

"I won't touch anything, I promise. I may use that mirror on the wall to touch myself up, if that's alright?"

Cullens hesitated for another moment, before nodding. "Fine. I won't be long."

As soon as he stepped outside of the room, Irene shivered,

trying to shake off the feeling of his finger on her face. While she enjoyed physical contact – when she gave it – she rarely enjoyed it from outsiders. Miss Hudson, and her close friends like Henriette and Jeannie were allowed a hug, but the only male touch she'd been able to tolerate was Eddy's brotherly affection, and whenever she connected with Joe.

But those were men she liked. Of course, there was a possibility of her liking another man enough to let him touch her, but for now, she'd keep her disdain for contact.

She shook her shoulders and marvelled at the fact that little womanly attributes went this far as to manipulate a supposedly intelligent man.

She scooped up all the files that would fit into her bag, paying special mind to get Olivia's and June's. Once finished, she slung the strap across her shoulder and headed to the office door.

She peered out into the hallway, but it was all clear. Keeping the bag close, Irene walked briskly, stepping only on her toes to lessen the sound she made. She slipped down the side hallway, toward the staircase that would take her down to reception.

She made it to the stairs, running down as fast as she could. Hopefully she could peruse these files quick enough and return them without too much fallout. She opened the door to the main floor and slowed her steps ever-so-slightly. She tried to walk with ease, as if her bag wasn't loaded down with government secrets.

She kept her head down as she strode out of the building, but couldn't help the grin that spread across her face.

Cullens would learn a hard lesson today.

Chapter VIII
Cutting Connections in the Government

Joe sipped at his tea as he checked the clock. He had no idea how long Irene would be away. He wished he'd gone with her. Cullens was a persistent man who clearly liked her. Just how far would he push, especially if he got Irene in a room alone? Though, no doubt Irene could handle herself, it wasn't right that she should even have to think that way.

The front door downstairs banged open and his flatmate thudded up the steps in a hurry.

Joe stood, ready for whatever she had brought back.

She entered the room looking less frantic than her footsteps suggested.

"Joe, we must go. I have files to be read but we must study them elsewhere."

His heart rate immediately sped up. He tried to remain calm and figure out if this was really cause to panic or if his partner was simply excited.

"Miss Hudson has just made tea." He gestured to the table to get her to sit and explain things. "Why can't we read them here? Have you discovered a thinking spot in some cosy nest of London that helps you ponder better?"

The tea and biscuits worked for a second, but didn't have enough swaying power in the end.

"No place helps me ponder better than Baker Street. These files are just sensitive and people may–"

Joe's eyes widened. "Oh Irene. What did you do?"

"Cullens wasn't particularly forthcoming, so I took it upon myself–"

"Irene..."

"This is important," she huffed. "There is a mystery behind June's death, and an address for Olive Bennet."

Joe paused his chastising. Those were two major breaks in the case.

"And he was hiding those from you?"

"Yes." She opened each folder, laying them on the table. "We argued, he refused to give me anything; even went as far as to threaten me. And… I may have flirted to get him to bring the files I needed into his office, then feigned a sore throat. I ran off with the files when he went to fetch tea."

"Oh, good lord!" Joe dropped his head in his hand. "Irene, you just made an enemy out of a gov—Wait, he threatened you?"

She waved him off. "Veiled at best. Trying to be intimidating."

He shouldn't have been surprised. Irene perpetuated these types of scenarios all the time. But this was one that could land them in serious trouble should Cullens take action.

"He's going to come looking for these files, isn't he?"

"Potentially."

"And are we going to give them back?"

"If we are finished with them."

"And if we aren't?"

"We deny everything."

Joe nodded as he stared at the folder. "I was afraid you'd say that. Let's look through these quick before we're both arrested."

Irene dragged the chair beside him and patted his shoulder. "I wouldn't let them arrest you, Joe."

"I'm not letting anyone arrest *you*."

"Then there is nothing for us to worry about."

She pulled the folder toward her and opened it. As nervous as he was with the stolen documents on the table, he wasn't surprised, and was even less worried than he should be. Perhaps almost a whole year with Irene was wearing off on him and he knew some things were for the better.

Or perhaps it was because he was now actively working a case and didn't feel guilty for avoiding Sarah.

Irene immediately grabbed June's file, skimming the

information quickly before slapping the paper down.

"She is our author, Joe. The handwriting in the book matches notes she'd written in her file and her signature. Look at the loops and dips."

"This does look similar. But why would she write these names down? Surely she wasn't killing these women."

"Perhaps she was simply trying to track them down. Continue reading Olivia's file. I'm going to dig deeper into June."

Joe took the woman's file and immediately found two London addresses she could be living at. Smiling at their quick luck, he set the folder down.

"Irene, I found where–"

"Oh dear." Her dark eyes were wide as they flew across the page. He'd rarely seen her, if at all, disturbed by anything pertaining to cases. Irene finally met his eyes.

"June didn't kill herself," she said, voice wavering for a brief second. "There were signs that she'd been tortured. Bruises and cuts upon her body. Apparently a government agent did show up after the police found her, given who she was. They covered it up, though, ruling it a suicide."

She flipped the file to him. Pictures flashed of an autopsy of a beaten woman with slash marks through her wrists. Joe looked away, stomach turning.

"But why?"

Irene stood to pace. "Why was she tortured? For this book

perhaps. Was the man who keeps breaking into Sarah's house the same man who hurt her? Most likely. Is he looking for this in order to potentially kill the rest of these women? I assume so."

"But why would the government cover it up?"

"To not incite panic. If word got out that a woman was tortured, then it might have been obvious she used to be a spy. Or perhaps they didn't want to alert any other agencies that she'd been found out."

"Do we tell her brother?"

"I don't know yet. Let's see what becomes of this case."

She slid back into the chair, taking another folder. Her gaze darkened, turning angry as she handed him the papers she read.

"Carrie Harrison. Look how she was killed. In the same way, except they didn't stage it as a suicide."

Luckily, the autopsy photos were on the following page. This one listed the brutal attack, including a severe beating and other horrific acts that churned Joe's stomach.

He immediately wanted to call home to check on his sisters and tell them to never go near a man ever again.

Irene snatched the file from him. "I'm sorry, Joe. I shouldn't have shown you."

"I appreciate that," Joe said. "But it comes with the job, I suppose."

"Unfortunately."

Joe pulled himself back, his stomach still a bit queasy. He wasn't so much reacting to the gore, but the fact that two young women were brutalized for some secrets.

It was despicable what the war did to everyone.

"Joe?" Irene touched his arm. "I would offer you a minute to collect yourself, but we may not have the time."

"I am fine," he assured his friend. "This case just took a turn, as they all seem to do."

She accepted his answer, but still moved her hand down gently into his. "Of the two addresses you found for Olivia, one of them matches up."

One of the addresses in the book was the same as in the government file.

"This address cannot get out." Irene dropped Joe's hand, standing. "If anyone finds out, they will seek out Olivia and potentially harm her. Obviously, the book cannot leave us, but the file…"

She trailed off and Joe tried to keep up with her thought process as she held the papers. What did the sometimes-impetuous sleuth do in times of duress? He stood, grabbing the file from her hands.

"We cannot destroy this. It is a classified government document! Not a police report only going to Lestrade."

However, Irene wasn't listening. She hurried to her desk, Joe on her heels. When she grabbed for a pen, he snatched it away.

He held it above his head as she jumped for it in what was probably the most ridiculous scene.

"Joe!" She snapped. "I just need to blackout the address. We have to keep this woman safe. Please!"

The desperation in her voice made him lower the pen. "You are that concerned?"

She took the pen from him, and when she spoke, her voice was low and worried. "You saw what they did to June. I am assuming it was our culprit, but who knows what Cullens and his friends are capable of."

"What if they are using this address to watch her and keep her safe?"

"If they don't already have tabs on her – or have not memorized her address by heart if they are indeed protecting her – then they are doing a lousy job. I cannot risk it."

Joe couldn't argue, nor could he stop her. The logic was sound. And if something like crossing off an address would help, then by all means.

Irene made tiny circles and loops with the pen as she blacked out the lines with the woman's address until it was gone.

"Not perfect, but it will do in a pinch."

Joe watched her with fascination, thinking back over the case.

"You know, for someone who said she doesn't understand the social cues of women, you certainly are very protective over them."

She set the pen down and sighed. "Women saved me during the war. Sure, Eddy played his part, but it was his sister, along with Jeannie and her girls, that kept me alive."

"I'd like to hear the story of how you came to know Jeannie sometime."

She straightened, all memories gone. "And you shall. But, now, let's finish with these folders, then I'll attempt to get them back to Cullens."

A mere five minutes later, they began packing up. Joe had never read so fast in his life.

They'd found the addresses for the other women marked *ALIVE* and Irene had scribbled them onto the paper beside their names. She then had blacked them out in the file. Most of them were out of the country; some in Scotland and one had moved to America.

"How are you going to get these back to Cullens?"

A sharp, loud knock came from downstairs, followed by the doorbell, then a knock again.

"Like that," Irene stated.

She tucked the folders under her arms and headed to the stairs.

Joe didn't know what compelled him to grab her arm.

"Wait. Maybe I will speak with him."

She thought about the idea for a second before nodding. "Probably a good idea. He will be quite mad at me."

"Exactly. And I don't trust angry men right now."

Irene stood in his eyeline, forcing his gaze to her. "You seem to be an angry man right now."

"Exactly."

The loud knock sounded again, sharper, angrier.

Joe felt his blood pressure rise. He hated any sort of confrontation, and this was the exact definition of it. But he felt compelled again. He needed to make sure Irene was safe.

He hurried down the stairs, pulse quickening. Hopefully the words came easily and he could dissuade Cullens from entering the house.

Joe had no idea what he would do if the man did decide to enter. Though he was taller, Cullens was broader and probably had special training.

He opened the door and sure enough, the man of the hour stood there in a suit and slicked hair. He smiled at Joe, but the expression was brimming with annoyance and aggravation.

"Ah, Dr. Watson. May I come in?"

"I'm afraid not," Joe said, gathering his courage. "We are in the middle of a case and must be left undisturbed." He held out his hand. "But I believe these belong to you."

"Ah, yes. These walked out of my office when I went to fetch a cup of tea."

"Well, now you have them back. We were on our way to return them, actually."

The man sighed but didn't move from the foyer. "May I speak

to Miss Holmes?"

Joe did his best to study him as Irene would. Now that he had his folders, he should've departed, yet remained on the front step.

Joe remembered all the flowers he'd sent to Irene, and how she had avoided seeing him or going to dinner with him over the winter months.

This man wasn't here about the folders, not really. He was here to speak with Irene on personal matters.

A strange feeling stirred within him again, like nausea and anger all at once. It was small, but powerful all the same.

"Irene is busy. She cannot speak to you right now, but I shall pass on any message you would like to send."

"She's been busy for a while. In fact, I've never met a woman so desperate to be doing other things than even see me."

Joe shrugged, the small ball in his stomach fuelling his adrenaline. "Then perhaps you should sniff around elsewhere."

His words came out sharp and fierce, and he immediately regretted them. He didn't like confrontation, or fights, or even loud voices. Now, he was face to face with a man double his stature, with large fists that could probably throw a punch or two.

But there was the primal need to defend his home and his friend who, if given the chance, would only make things worse anyway.

The agent sighed and stepped close, giving the illusion of trust. "Look, if she is seeing someone else, then…"

"She isn't seeing anyone, and she shouldn't have to just to keep men from pursuing her."

Joe had no idea where this newfound courage was coming from, but he couldn't stop.

Cullens face reddened. He kept looking past Joe, as if the object of his desires would materialize at the top of the stairs and float down to him.

He stepped even closer.

"Whatever arrangement she has here with you, she can have just as good, if not better with me. I will take her off your hands and keep her satisfied. Isn't that what you're doing here?"

The little ball of adrenaline finally split open.

"What you are implying is out of line. You need to step out of *my* house at once. You have your folders, now leave."

Cullens didn't budge. His face turned red as a tomato and his fists clenched. "I could have you both arrested."

"Go on and ring Scotland Yard, then." Joe's heart hammered in his chest, his palms sweating like mad. But he'd gone too far now and needed to continue holding his ground.

"Your woman came into my office, promised me some very suggestive things, then stole from me. I'd like to–"

"It is not my fault that you fell for one of the oldest tricks in the book. Clearly, you aren't as desirable as you think you are, and yet your ego is inflated enough that a simple rouse fooled you."

Regret washed over Joe. How was he so bold? These were the type of quick-thinking insults that Irene usually quipped. He thought about stuttering an apology before shutting the door on Cullens. He almost opened his mouth to do so, but the man stepped forward, keeping his voice low.

"Keep her, then. She's a bit of a bitch and I doubt she would've done me any favours."

He could take all the insults in the world. Hell, he could take all the beatings in the world. But if this man thought he could insult Irene and pass her around like some possession, then he was gravely mistaken.

As if on automatic, Joe wound his fist back and swung. Skin met bone, making a crunching sound. Blood instantly poured from Cullens' nose.

"You bastard, you broke my bloody nose!" he cried through his fingers. "You're mad. All of you."

Joe's knuckles stung with the impact. He shook his hand, moving his fingers to lessen the pain. Yet he stayed at the ready, in case this vile man wanted a round two.

However, Cullens turned on his heels and marched out, head tilted back to stop the blood.

"Good heavens!" Miss Hudson's panicked voice came from the hall.

"What is going on?"

Joe's heart raced so fast that it almost made him dizzy. "Don't fret, Miss Hudson. Everything is alright now."

Hopefully, at least. He doubted Cullens would be back any time soon.

The landlady rushed to look at his hand. "You've cut your knuckle. It'll need cleaning."

Joe tried to tell her he'd be fine, but was interupted by Irene's voice from the top of the stairs.

"I will take care of him, Miss Hudson."

Even though he felt like his knees would give out at any moment, he made it up the stairs and to the dining table. His friend soaked a cloth in cold water and held it to his knuckles that were swelling already.

"How much did you hear?"

"Oh, I didn't miss a word." Irene smirked up at him as she patted his knuckles.

Joe's cheeks heated up. "I apologize on his behalf."

She snorted. "If you apologized for everyone who made nasty comments about me, then your tongue would be sore."

"Does it bother you when people make those assumptions?"

She sat back in the chair and shrugged. "No. I know what I am and I know what my situation is. I dislike it when they make assumptions about my intelligence or my capabilities, but if there are people out there who think me odd for not taking a husband yet, or for the living arrangement here, then let them. I do not want to associate with such people anyway. I do apologize that I don't make it easier for you, though."

"Oh, goodness, Irene. That's not what I meant. It's not your job to dictate how I feel."

"No, but as your friend, it is my job to help you." She stood to put more water on the cloth. "Though, I will admit, it did feel quite nice having a knight-in-shining-armour defend me."

Joe grinned, looking down at his swollen hand. "You did it for me when I was kidnapped last year."

"Ha!" She handed him the cloth. "I stumbled into a warehouse in a drug-filled stupor waving a gun around. It was a miracle I didn't shoot you."

Joe remembered the whole ordeal in glaring detail. It seemed so long ago, especially with the winter they had.

He quickly sobered up, recalling what he'd read in those files. "I just can't imagine what those women went through, and sometimes, the cases we work on... If you…"

Irene scooted the chair right next to his and took both his hands. "You silly man. I am more than capable–"

"What if you're not?"

She took his face instead, forcing him to look at her. "That is why I have you. You're my partner. I know I am safe if you are here. And though your punches could use a bit of work, that was a solid hit."

Irene released him, but his cheeks stayed warm.

He'd have to contemplate what she'd said later; her words triggered a new panic in him that was about to force him to rethink some major choices — namely ones with Sarah.

"Right," Irene smacked the table. "Time to put this case to bed once and for all."

"How?" Joe stood, resetting himself. He tossed the wet cloth in the laundry hamper.

"The names in here are precious." She held up the book. "And now that we know they were spies, it puts their lives at risk. The ones still alive, that is."

"So, what do we do? Everyone is looking for that book."

A sly grin spread over Irene's face.

Joe sighed. "I just got through defending you from the trouble you caused."

"When am I not in trouble?" She grinned wider. "I have a plan."

"Is it a good plan?"

She pondered for a second, then shrugged. "It is going to get some knickers in some knots."

"Oh, Irene..."

"Don't worry. You've already proven you can usurp Cullens once. You'll be fine." She walked into her bedroom before he could respond.

While Joe didn't feel exactly triumphant socking a government agent, the soft look on Irene's face, however, was something he had never seen before. She looked vulnerable, grateful...and simply lovely.

He halted his thoughts like car brakes and looked around, as if there were someone able to read his mind. Clearing his throat, he shook his head, attempting to drive his head back to the mystery at hand.

Anxious to finish the case, he couldn't wait to inact Irene's plan, no matter how worrisome it may be.

Chapter IX

The Names Are Gone for Good

A little over an hour after the incident with Cullens, Irene stood with the telephone pressed to her ear.

"DI Lestrade," said a tired voice on the other end.

"Edward, my dear."

"What did you do?"

"Nothing."

Joe looked up from his chair, eyebrow quirked.

Irene turned from him and continued her conversation.

"What are you *about* to do?" Eddy asked, but the caring undertone of his voice told Irene he was already onboard with whatever her plan was.

"I am about to close this case."

"You've figured out who the man is?"

"Of course," she said. "And I am going to lure him out."

"What did he want anyway? What was in that book you

found?"

"Names of all the women spies during the war."

"Oh heavens. Why doesn't your chap from the government take this on?"

"Funny you should mention him," Irene said, peering at Joe, who still sat with a curious look on his face. "We have been in touch actually. And I would like you to ring him up and let him know the plan I am about to relay to you."

"Why can't you call him? It's you that has the relationship with him."

"Its complicated. Tell him, that if he wants to catch himself a former Nazi spy, he needs to follow our instructions exactly."

* * * * *

That evening, the pair waited in the back garden of Sarah's house. Joe paced around, clearly nervous about the prospect of meeting Cullens again.

"Relax, Joe. Eddy, Thom, and I will all be here, should he think to attack you or verbally assault me."

She'd suggested to Eddy to invite Thom along, mostly because the DI was quite good at calming people down. It never worked on her, of course, but she'd seen him in action plenty of times. Also, one government agent against two Scotland Yard DI's, plus her and Joe, would hopefully deter any antics he might attempt.

Muffled steps came from the side of the house. The two detectives turned the corner, meeting Joe and Irene in the weeds.

Thom made a point of looking around. "We did this once before, did we not? During that dog case?"

Irene nodded. "It worked then, so why not now?"

More footsteps came. Agent Cullens entered the small garden.

Irene caught his very brief hesitation when he spotted Joe. Her lips tugged in a smile at how her soft, sweet friend caused a trained agent to second guess himself.

He introduced himself to Eddy and Thom, with the latter remarking on his tie. Then he looked at Irene.

"Miss Holmes," he said, words stiff. "Hopefully this plan of yours works."

"My plans always work out."

The agent touched the trellis that was trapped in ivy against the house. "Should we remove this? Direct this man where we want him?"

Irene immediately rejected the idea. "If he notices anything out of the ordinary, he may flee. Two of us will be upstairs, the rest downstairs."

Eddy checked his watch. "The girls should be leaving any minute."

Just then, the front door to the house closed. Giggles and chatter drifted throughout the street as Sarah and her friends made a show of leaving the house, talking about dancing all night.

They did exactly what Irene had instructed them to, and she couldn't have been more grateful for their cooperation.

The men, however, were a different story. Hopefully they respected her plan as much as the ladies did.

"Come, gentlemen," she commanded, entering through the back door. "Joe and I will take the upstairs, the three of you will wait in the shadows down here. And do remember to wait until this man is completely in the house and you've blocked his exit. I do not feel like pursuing anyone on foot tonight."

She didn't wait for them to argue back as she made her way up the stairs, Joe at her heels. They opted to wait in Jenny and Dottie's room. Should this man come through the lavatory window like he had the other night, he'd walk past them to Sarah's room, then they could pursue while blocking him in.

Joe leaned against the wall just inside the door. Meanwhile, Irene perched on the floor, cross-legged.

And they waited.

* * * * *

Nearly two hours later, Irene opened her eyes. She hadn't been asleep by any means, merely meditating until she heard a sound. She couldn't say the same for Joe, who's steady, slow breathing told her–

"I'm not asleep," he said as if reading her mind. "I am simply trying your trick of relaxing and listening."

"You didn't fall asleep at all?" she teased. "Not even once?"

"'Course not," he yawned. "We're on a case."

Irene stood silently and shuffled closer to him. "You think the others fell asleep?"

She didn't get her answer though.

The back door downstairs gave the smallest creak. A moment of silence followed. Irene almost thought it had been Thom, Eddy, or Cullens slipping out for a pee break.

Then, scuffling on the wood and Thom shouting. A loud thud struck the wood in the downstairs hallway, and more shouting echoed through the house.

Irene flung the bedroom door open and raced downstairs with Joe close behind.

She skidded to a halt at the bottom step, causing Joe to crash into her as they took in the scene in the front hall.

Eddy lay on the ground, clutching his side. Thom and Cullens were locked in hand-to-hand combat with the large angry stranger in a thick coat. He threw Thom to the side like a ragdoll and the DI crumpled to the ground. The government agent dodged a few punches and got a strike in, but the man barely flinched.

Joe went to join the fight, but Irene grabbed his arm. He'd

only get hurt if he intervened. She pushed him into the living room and out of the way.

Eddy bounced back to his feet and swung, catching the man in the side. Cuss words and pained grunts echoed in the air as the men started into another grappling session.

In the fray, their culprit pulled something shiny from his jacket. He managed to back away, aiming a gun at Eddy.

He shouted something in German.

Cullens drew his own weapon.

At this rate, someone was bound to get shot. Irene didn't much care if Cullens got a bullet through him, but she'd be damned if Eddy, or even Thom, ended up injured.

Pulling a box of matches from her pocket, she lit one and chucked it into the fireplace. It roared to life, lighting the whole first floor.

Unfortunately, the distraction was not big enough to sway the action. Desperate times, then.

Irene pulled the leatherbound dark book from her bag.

She saw Joe panic in her peripherals. "What are you–"

"Gentlemen!" All four turned as she stood dangling the book over the fire.

"Weapons down, or I will drop this."

Both Cullens and the culprit yelled in unison, "No!"

"Then I suggest you lower the weapons."

But no one moved.

She gritted her teeth and moved the book closer to the flames.

Eddy slowly backed away from the line of fire, close to Thom, who grabbed his partners arm in exhaustion.

With everyone's attention now on her, Irene commanded the room. "You, sir, what is your name?"

He spat some German at her.

"In English. We all know you can speak it."

"We do?" Thom asked, injured but still very curious.

"Of course. I believe he worked alongside Agent Cullens here for a short while during the war."

At this revelation, the agent lowered his weapon and stepped forward to see the man's face. "Good lord. Robert?"

The man – Robert – glanced at his former partner, then back at Irene. She continued to speak.

"A gruff south London accent would be easy for anyone to learn if they put their mind to it. And to infiltrate the government when it was all mixed up during the war wouldn't have been hard. But then finding out that your own country was being infiltrated by the enemy – by women, no less – would've made anyone mad. Especially if you'd worked so hard getting the location of a few high-ranking British officers that led to their capture. It's amazing what one woman can do when she puts her mind to it; including rescuing that group you worked so hard to capture.

"When you found the address of the woman who'd defeated

you, you kidnapped her – or so you thought. You'd taken Carrie instead, later torturing her to find out June's location. But she was on to you; she started this list to protect all the other women you might come after. And then you beat her into telling you the information too. But what you didn't account for was that June was strong enough to endure your torture without divulging anything. Thus, your search for this book began. Am I on the right track, Robert?"

Silence filled the room as everyone waited for the large man's answer. He glared at Irene and she stared back, willing him to speak and daring him to attack.

He finally spat at her. "There were dozens of them. And they were ruining it all. They shouldn't even be allowed to walk the streets, and yet here they were, ruining the grand plan."

The man's chest rose up and down in heavy, angry breaths. His German accent slipped, but he'd spoken English for so long, there was no getting rid of the southern accent either.

From behind him, Thom spat a horrid curse word and Eddy had to hold him back. Cullens stepped forward and kicked the back of Robert's knees. The culprit dropped to the ground and Eddy held out a pair of handcuffs. The government agent exchanged them for Robert's gun and Eddy kept the man under aim as he cuffed him.

"The grand plan crashed and burned," Irene said. "You lost once, and you've lost once again. Though what you deserve is everything you did to June and Carrie."

Robert spat at their names.

Irene lowered the book and walked toward him, her fingers forming a fist. She was exhausted and after reading about what this man had done to those women, and who knew how many others, she couldn't make peace with him going to jail in one piece and a smirk on his lips.

She struck Robert, cracking his nose and her knuckles in the process. If Cullens wanted to stop her, he made no motion of it. The man went down hard though, and the agent let him fall to the ground with a thump.

Once he was down, Irene moved back, taking up her place between Joe and the fireplace once more.

With Eddy still pointing the gun at their culprit – who clearly was not going anywhere – Cullens turned his attention to Irene.

"The book please, Miss Holmes," he said, palm out. "Then I will take this man away."

She hesitated.

Beside her, Joe muttered. "Irene, please. Let this be over."

"You're right," she said, then turned to the roaring fire. She dropped the book into the flames.

"No!" Cullens leaped forward into the living room as the fire engulfed the book, the pages crackling. "What are you doing?"

"No one needs it."

The agent was speechless, torn between staying with his

prisoner and attempting to rescue whatever was left.

Joe shuffled closer to Irene, holding out a protective arm should he advance.

Thom stepped past Eddy who still held Robert at gun point.

"I think we are all done here. Agent Cullens, take your prisoner. Lestrade and I can escort you to wherever you wish to transport him."

Cullens hesitated as he looked between the flames and his former love interest, but eventually resigned and lifted Robert to his feet. He gave a final look to Irene and she hoped it meant no more flowers.

Thom followed him out, leaving Eddy to linger for a moment.

"I hope that was the right call," he said, gesturing to the fire. "For all our sakes."

Irene's stomach still churned from what she'd read. "If you knew what he did, you wouldn't let him make it to prison."

"That's not my call," Eddy said, placing his arm on her shoulder. "And it's not yours either. I'm sure he will get his due in the long run."

He kissed her cheek and moved away.

Joe took his place, wrapping his arm around Irene's shoulder.

"Will we have to give any statements?"

Eddy shrugged. "It's in the government's hands now, and from the looks of your knuckles, Cullens' broken nose and this stunt Irene just pulled, I doubt he will want to speak to either of you anytime soon. Though, the next time I'm round at Baker Street, I expect to hear *that* story."

"It's quite an epic tale," Irene winked. "And I will gladly paint Joe as the hero he is. Now, we shall wait until Sarah and her friends are home to explain things to them, then we will go home and get some much-needed sleep."

"Jolly good," Eddy said, then headed out of the house.

Once the pair were alone in the living room, Joe sunk into the sofa and buried his face in his hands.

"I can't believe, after all that, you simply tossed the book into the fire."

Irene bounced on her feet. "Oh Joe. You don't really think that was the real book, do you?"

Joe looked up at her, exhaustion and disbelief written all over his face. His mouth opened, but it was as if he'd gone mute.

"Now, shall I make a cuppa while we wait for Sarah?"

* * * * *

The following day, Irene walked down a lovely quiet street at the edge of the city. They didn't go into much detail when they relied the previous night's happenings to Sarah and her friends. After that, as promised, the pair left to go back to Baker Street for some much needed sleep.

Irene had departed the flat earlier this morning while Joe

snored away in his bedroom. Sarah had phoned just before she left to thank them again. The two ladies had a lovely little chat before Sarah had to leave for work.

Once Irene hung up, she realized that she'd made yet another friend. She truly was collecting them like shiny trinkets.

The target of her quest appeared in view. She was looking at a quaint house with a tidy front garden. Straightening her hat and tucking her curls, Irene took a deep breath and knocked on the door.

A woman not much older than her answered. There was a small scar on her cheekbone.

She immediately gave Irene a once-over.

"Can I help you?"

"My name is Irene Holmes. I am a private investigator and I have something for you, if you've got a moment."

The woman hesitated, then stepped back and let Irene into her home.

"You are Olivia Bennet."

The woman stiffened as she took Irene's hat and gloves.

"You must be confusing me with someone else."

Irene dug into the pocket of her jacket and noted that Olivia kept a sharp watch on her hands. Rather than a weapon, like the woman was expecting, she pulled out a photograph.

Olivia took the photo and paled. "How…"

"Hubert Harriott. If we may sit, please. I have more."

Five minutes later, they were in a cosy sitting area. Olivia had no pictures up; no family running about either. Despite her lovely home, she shared her life with no one.

"We found the man who killed Carrie and June, among others," Irene began. "We came across this as a result."

She held out the leatherbound notebook from her bag.

Olivia took the item with shaky hands, flipping it open. "This belonged to June."

Irene nodded. "The man in question was searching houses for where June must've hid it—"

"I hid it," Olivia interrupted. "June never let me know what was in it. Then, one day, she gave it to me in a manic state and told me to hide it without telling her where. But then she walked in as I was stashing it."

"In the closet of your bedroom."

"Yes. She nearly lost her mind – whatever was left of it anyway. She told me to hide it elsewhere and that she couldn't know where it was. I convinced her it would be fine. But, in the end, it wasn't."

"I must tell you, she didn't kill herself… But I will not go into detail as it is one of the most gruesome accounts I have read."

Olivia huffed a tired, sad laugh. "I saw what happened to Carrie before they took her away. I assume June went through the same thing. In fact, I knew, as soon as I heard they'd found her body, that something was amiss. But I couldn't bring myself to get involved. I'd lost two friends already, and more during the war. My mind couldn't bear living through it again."

Irene nodded, suddenly solemn. "I lost people as well."

The woman didn't look up from the book as she spoke.

"They expect us to be strong, and when we're not, we are pushed away with the rest of the women."

"That statement is all too true."

"Do you take on many cases like these?"

"I try to," Irene sighed. "I attempt to solve cases the police dismiss, or the ones deemed too tricky and tossed away."

This gave Olivia pause. "A Holmes that solves odd cases. Like… Sherlock Holmes?"

Irene stiffened, but the usual panic whenever someone mentioned her father didn't come. She'd been getting better at handling mentions of her father, and was glad her body didn't revolt at this conversation.

"He is my father."

"I read his stories during training. If you are anything like him – and surely you must be to have brought me this – then we could've used a woman like you at Bletchley."

"Funny, I have been told that before."

Olivia gazed down at the book again. "I can't tell you what this means to me."

"There are no copies of the addresses. I defaced several government documents to ensure that."

"You would've fit right in with us, for sure." Olivia chuckled.

Irene didn't know where the sudden vulnerability came from – perhaps from the mention of her father, or a certain kinship she felt with this woman – but a thought popped onto the tip of her tongue.

"Sometimes I do wonder what it was all for. The whole war, us working so hard, and still to this day, pursuing crazy criminals in hopes to make the world a better place."

"Because we think the world is a good place, perhaps." Olivia turned her smile to Irene and there was such tenderness and kindness to it that it soothed her immediately.

"I've seen the underbelly. It is not."

"Then perhaps it's because we know it can be? And we have hope that one day we won't have to worry about war on our doorstep or the boogeyman in our closet."

"That sounds like a fanciful fantasy."

"Certainly. But it's one we are willing to fight for."

"The greater good?" Irene was turning sceptical.

Olivia must've seen it on her face because she laughed again.

"Day-by-day happiness. Not only ours, but the people we surround ourselves with. We achieve it by doing what we are good at and what makes us happy. And making sure the people we love know we love them."

The way she said the last line gave Irene pause.

"You know, Hubert Harriott resides in London. I may leave his address, if you wish."

Olivia pursed her lips, drumming her fingers on her lap. "He believes I am in America."

"Correct. But there's nothing to say you didn't come back. I will leave it, and you may do what you like."

"He hasn't taken a wife?"

Irene shook her head and stood. "Now, I shall get out of your hair."

The retired spy stood as well and walked her to the door.

Irene had heard Joe thank every soldier they'd spoken to and felt the urge to do so herself.

"Thank you," she said. "For everything you did during the war."

"And thank *you*," Olivia bowed her head. "For what you continue to do now."

They shook hands as if old friends.

As Irene headed to the car, she felt a lump in her throat. A strange swirl of emotions stirred inside her, mixing with the exhaustion, stinging her eyes. She wanted to go home and hide under a blanket until it went away. At the same time, she also wanted to go dancing – with Sarah and her friends, or just Joe – and revel in the post-war city London had become.

* * * * *

When she arrived home, she found Joe in his chair, still clad in pyjamas. He perked up when she entered the room, his hair wild and bags still under his eyes.

"There you are! Everything okay?"

"Of course. I just went for a morning drive."

She turned to the plate of still warm toast and helped herself.

"Are you going to say it?" Joe asked from behind her.

"What?"

"I told you so?"

Irene snorted, spraying toast crumbs. "I do not engage in such juvenile things. Though, next time I declare a mystery, perhaps you could take a moment to indulge me, lest there be something even more sinister."

She held out the last piece of toast for him.

"I promise," Joe said. "Next case I will hang on your every word and listen to your every command."

"That is all I ask, dear Joe. Oh, and I will be using the car next week. Sarah and the girls have invited me for tea. They wish to learn to be bolder."

His shoulders dropped as he bit the toast. "Oh Christ, Irene. You're going to start a revolution."

"As long as I can still work my cases, I don't care what I start. Also, I figured out what your problem is."

"Oh yes? Enlighten me."

"You are not happy. Not truly, anyway. I have no idea how to fix this, as I have seen glimpses of your true happiness, but cannot put together a correlation between them. So, you must figure out what makes you well and truly happy, Joe Watson. That's an order."

He stared at her as if he'd been accosted in the middle of his breakfast. "Well, I… I am…"

He trailed off and finished his toast instead. He was staring so hard at the table, it was a wonder a hole didn't magically appear in it.

Irene fed a piece of her crust to the dog then clasped her hands together. "Come, Isla, let's pop to the shops. I forgot to get the latest Edinburgh paper."

She secured her hat again and grabbed the dog leash. As she left the flat, she heard Joe call after her.

"And what makes you happy, Irene Holmes?"

Irene gestured around the room. "This. Baker Street. You and me. Cases. No more, no less."

She stopped to put a finger on her chin. "Well, perhaps also potatoes that weren't from a box, but those will come back."

Joe gave her a lopsided smile and a warm, loving look. He then pointed to his wallet on the telephone table. Catching it from where Irene had tossed it, he dug out some coins.

"For more Turkish Delights."

Irene grinned at him, snatching the money. "You're certain?"

"If it's going to make you grin like that, then buy as many as those coins will get you."

She wiggled her shoulders, already tasting the powdered sugar. "Come, Isla. Perhaps we will even stop by the butchers and get you a lovely bone. We will be back, my dear Joe. With sweets abound!"

Outside, the sun was peeking through the clouds and a slightly warm breeze blew past Irene as she walked. The winter had been dreadful, and London wasn't entirely recovered yet, but every day became a bit brighter. Hopefully this year brought even more cases and a chance for Irene and Joe to truly prove themselves as the strong duo she knew they were.

Of course, there would be struggles; she could already foresee a few arguments in terms of their living arrangement and Joe's future with Sarah, but they hadn't happened yet. That was a future problem to solve.

The coins jingled in her purse and the sweets shop was a block away. Together with Isla the terrier, they strutted happily along the street, while her best friend waited at home for whatever goodies Irene brought back.

THE END

HOLMES & CO. WILL RETURN IN:

THE MISSING TWO

When two young women go missing at a prestigious finishing school, Irene and Joe are requested to investigate the disappearance. Both students hail from wealthy families and where there's money — there's impatience and demand. But not all is as it seems behind the closed doors of these wealthy families. Soon, Irene and Joe are thrust into a world of feuding parents and secret pasts, and must try as hard as they can to keep their wits about them.

About the Author

Allison Osborne lives in Ontario, Canada with her son, their West Highland terrier, and an overwhelming amount of vintage trinkets. She attended the University of Western Ontario for creative writing, and when her mind isn't wandering through 1940s England, she's busy dabbling in scriptwriting and other grand adventures.

Connect with Allison

Instagram: @allisonoauthor

Web: www.aosborneauthor.com

Milton Keynes UK
Ingram Content Group UK Ltd.
UKHW051024230624
444490UK00010B/297